SCARRED

SINS AND SECRETS SERIES OF DUETS

WILLOW WINTERS

ABOUT

She made me a better man, but I still wasn't good enough to keep her.

Born and raised in Brooklyn, with full sleeve tattoos, ripped muscles and a coldhearted stare, I am who I am.

The bad boy she knew to stay away from.

It was a given that we were never supposed to last. But the way her lips tasted, the way her curves felt under my hands … I couldn't let go. I did everything I could to keep her.

I put a ring on her finger and straightened out my life. All for her.

I should've known better.

One mistake tore us apart and I don't know what I can do to salvage what we once had.

I knew it wasn't supposed to last, but if I could make her stay with me once ... I can do it again.

Watch me.

I love my wife; I'm not letting her go.

Love does not delight in evil but rejoices with the truth. It always protects, always trusts, always hopes, always perseveres. – 1 Corinthians 13

CHAPTER 1

Evan

Wedding vows sound so sweet,
Meant for times of joy.
The truth is so much darker,
Filled with moments to destroy.
Your sins left me broken,
Scared and lonely too.
With no one to hear my plea,
With a secret no one knew.

I PROMISE to love you forever. And that's the easy part.

To honor and cherish you.

To keep your wishes and dreams my own.

To comfort you and keep you safe, always.

Till death do us part.

MY WEDDING VOWS HAUNT ME. The parts of them that I can remember, at least. I can't stop seeing the look of complete devotion on Kat's face on our wedding day, as I read my vows from a scrap of paper I'd written them on.

My heart raced as I spoke each word, my gaze straying from the paper to look back at her. She was so beautiful, with a love that I knew I didn't deserve.

I can still remember the feel of her soft skin as I cupped her cheek in my hand. I can still smell the sweet fragrance that drifted toward me as I leaned closer to her, all of our friends and family clapping and cheering as I took my first kiss from my wife.

I can still taste her lips on mine.

When I said those words, I meant them. I thought they'd be so easy to keep, to be honest, and it never occurred to me that I'd forget.

A large metal door opens at the end of the hall and I look up, my view obstructed by steel bars from the jail cell.

It's been a long damn time since I've been locked up. Years. Almost a dozen years, to be exact. I knew I'd be back soon though.

It was only a matter of time before they brought me in for questioning. I sit hunched over, resting my forearms on my thighs as I wait for the attending officer to come get me. He walks right past me though and I drop my head, focusing on the concrete floor and recalling every detail of the night that put me here.

My hands sweat as I twist my wedding band around my finger. I can't think about Kat right now or what she'd say. I haven't told her a damn thing about this and she's still not letting me back into her life. If she knew the truth, she'd hate me forever.

The worst part about all of this, is that I don't have a way out yet. I'm just falling into a dark black hole, not knowing how to escape, or when it will even end.

Someone coughs and I slowly turn my head to the left where it came from a few cells down, but I can't see a damn thing. I think there's only one other person in holding with me. And he's on the same side so the rest of the cells are empty. I guess Tuesdays are slow days for the station.

My foot tap, tap, taps on the ground as I anxiously wait. The cops haven't given me shit to go on yet. Other than the word *murder*. My best guess is that they think I gave Tony the coke and knew it was laced with poison.

Even if I didn't know it was tainted, I'd still be held accountable. At least here in the state of New York I am. But that shit was fucked with. Someone *wanted* him dead. Although the only two people who knew it was even there were me and my old boss.

That lying piece of shit. My shoulders rise with a heavy breath as the anger gets the best of me. I can see him smile as he patted my back, walking out the room after making sure it'd be ready for our client, Tony. I know he knew.

He's the one who put it there. The only question I have on my mind, is whether or not he's the one who laced it. I can't imagine he did. He wouldn't be that stupid. But I'm not taking the fall for murder over that shitty decision that cost Tony his life.

"Thompson," the cop's voice bellows and echoes off the walls of the small cell.

"That's me," I answer him, looking him square in the eyes. I don't recognize him as he puts the key in the lock and opens the door wide for me to get out and walk to the interrogation room. Adrenaline pumps hard in my blood. It seems more intense now than it did years ago.

Maybe it's because I don't know how I'll get out of this. I have an alibi, but if James, my ex-boss, showed them the pictures proving I was with Tony that night, then I'm fucked.

I have to wonder if he would though. If that's the case, he was deliberately withholding evidence and they'd have to question his intentions and his involvement.

My boots smack against the floor and I walk at an easy pace, making sure I don't do anything to piss off the cop. He's a short guy. Probably in his thirties I guess. Lots of wrinkles around his eyes though. Maybe from the stress, maybe from the sun.

"After you," he says with a grim look on his face as he opens the door. I give him a nod and walk in; he doesn't follow me though.

I only hesitate to sit down for a moment. There are two men in the room already. A tall cop with broad shoulders and a thin mustache that I want to shave off and Jay McCann, the lawyer from James' PR company.

"You're fired," I tell him the second I sit down. I don't even look at the dumb fuck. He's represented me and plenty of other clients before, but I know he'd break attorney-client privilege and tell James everything. I don't trust him.

"Are you sure?" the cop asks me as McCann stutters over a response. Obviously shocked and I don't blame him.

"Evan, I don't understand. I highly suggest we talk about this before you-"

"Yes, I'm sure. Sorry, Jay." I turn to face him and wait for a response, but he stands up and straightens his jacket. He clenches his jaw as he grabs his briefcase and I can see he wants to say something, but he holds it in.

I watch him walk around the table and exit without another word, leaving me alone with the cop.

"I'm Detective Bradshaw, Mr. Thompson."

"I would say it's nice to meet you, but ... " I say with a smirk and tilt my hands up. Detective Bradshaw doesn't laugh or respond to my little joke. And that's fine. They never do in here where it's recorded. I know how this works.

"Have you been informed of your rights?"

"I have," I answer him.

"And do you know what you're being charged with?" he asks me.

"Charged?" I answer quickly, my back stiffening as my muscles tense. "I wasn't informed that I was being charged."

"Well, I imagine there's no refuting it on your part. You supplied Tony Lewis with the cocaine he overdosed on."

"And you want me to admit to handing over the cocaine to him so you have someone behind bars to take the fall for a hotshot's death?" I ask him sarcastically, seamlessly hiding how my nerves want to crack and how my blood pounds in my ears. I let out an uneasy huff of a laugh and shake my head. Leaning back in my seat I look him in the eyes with a smile as I say, "That's not happening, Detective."

"Well, someone is going to go down for murder, yes. But you'd only be sentenced for your part and we're willing to cut you a deal. Whoever laced it with strychnine intended for it to kill. There's no doubt in the DA's mind that it's murder."

He waits for a reaction, but I use every ounce of energy in me to not give him anything. I won't say a word. Inside, I'm denying it. No fucking way. There's no way James would give a client something that would kill him. They're wrong.

"We know it's someone within the firm. It's not the first time one of NY PR's clients has turned up dead." He leans back and adds, "As I'm sure you're aware."

As he talks, he pulls out a manila folder that was sitting

on his lap and tosses it my way. It lands with a heavy thud in front of me and I easily open it, feigning disinterest.

"Nothing points to that person being you, but this was intentional. Someone wanted whoever it was that was going to be taking this coke to die. It was laced with enough strychnine to kill with the smallest sample."

I don't say anything as he pauses. He points his finger to a chart. "Whoever did it wanted even the smallest dose to kill."

My heart beats hard in my chest and then again.

"If you have any information on how we'd go about finding the killer, that'd be useful and we'd certainly be grateful for that."

I have to calmly exhale a few times, keeping as still as possible and making sure my expression doesn't change in the least before I can respond. "I really liked Tony and it's a shame what happened to him. It's extremely upsetting to think someone murdered him."

"It is, especially since he didn't have any enemies we can find," the cop says and then leans forward.

"You know if we can't find who did it, you'll be taking the full brunt of things."

I let a sarcastic laugh rock my shoulders and then look

toward the door to my left. The one that leads to my freedom. "I'm sorry Detective, everyone I know loved Tony and I didn't give him any drugs." I lean forward, mimicking his posture as I add, "It's illegal."

"If that's the way you want to play it," he says, reaching for the folder and I lean back in my seat again as he collects the papers.

"Am I free to go now?" I ask him. "I'd like to leave."

He stands abruptly, making the steel chair legs scrape noisily across the floor. "I don't think so. Maybe a night in the cells will help you remember something."

Fucking prick.

"Be back in a bit, Thompson."

I clench my jaw and crack my knuckles as I watch him leave.

It's only when the door shuts and I'm left alone in the room that I realize the extent of what Detective Bradshaw said.

Someone wanted to kill Tony, knowing I'd give the coke to him. Maybe even thinking I'd take it too. I'm known for partying. It's why clients chose me to represent them in the firm. My head spins as I try to recount that night. There's no way anyone else could have gone in there. James had a key, and he gave me the only other copy.

I was there to party with the clients and make sure they had a good time, but stayed out of trouble. It was easy enough in the rec room.

For the last ten minutes I've been thinking someone was trying to kill Tony. It's what the detective was suggesting.

I'd bet anything that James thought I'd take a hit at least.

Maybe it's paranoia, but as I sit alone in the room, all I can think is that the coke was never intended for Tony.

Someone wanted me dead.

CHAPTER 2

Kat

You said you'd love me forever,
But forever was too long.

UNTITLED

You said I was your one true love,
But the two of us were wrong.
It's deceit and lies that broke us,
And living life in pain.
Forever was supposed to be ours,
But forever was said in vain.

It's not every day you read about your husband going to jail in the papers. That's one way to find out, I guess.

My heels click on the sidewalk as I make my way down to the end of the block so I can get home. The bags from the grocery on the corner dig into my arm.

It hurts after a few blocks, but I don't care. I let the pain sink in and focus on the front door to my townhouse.

It doesn't take long for my gaze to break.

Standing in front of the building, dressed in all blue and complete with the cap, is a female cop. She's short and blonde, with her hair pulled back into a low bun. My steps slow as I spot her and I want to break down again.

If only I'd stayed holed up in the apartment and didn't have to eat. The thought is bitter and I push myself to walk forward. Each step hurts more and more.

I must still love the asshole, 'cause knowing he's in trouble hurts down to my core.

It was the sign that I was looking for though. The one that put the nail in the coffin to my marriage.

"Mrs. Thompson," the cop says as I walk up to the stone steps.

"Hello," I say awkwardly. Not wanting to even look her in the eyes as the shame creeps up and makes the cold air feel even colder.

"I'm Detective Nicoli," the woman says and I nod my head, feeling the pinch of the plastic bags dig even deeper into my forearm as I shift on my feet.

"How can I help you, Detective?" I ask her and force myself to straighten my shoulders.

"Could I come in?" she asks me, as if I'd let her.

"I'd rather not," I answer, my voice a bit harsh. I struggle with the bags slightly, hearing them crinkle as I let out a low sigh. "It's been a long few days," I tell her.

"The bags under your eyes could have told me that," she says with no sympathy in her tone.

I huff out, "Thanks," with the intention of walking right by her and into the townhouse, but then she adds, "I'm sorry for what you're going through."

And I hesitate.

I stand there, taking it. Taking the sympathy but more than that, needing it. Tears burn my eyes as I look back at her. "What do you want?" I ask her.

"It would be better for you if I could come in?" she suggests, looking pointedly at the bags on my arm.

I shake my head. That's not happening.

The charge is murder if the papers are telling the truth.

I'm not interested in hearing from anyone other than my husband.

"Just ask me whatever you want," I tell her and lick my lower lip.

"I know you two are getting a divorce," she starts and the article from two days ago flashes in my memory.

All about how Evan lost his job, his wife and now he's being charged with murder. My heart twists just the same as it did when I read it.

"I wanted to know if you had any information at all that you'd like to give us," Detective Nicoli says and I shake my head, not trusting myself to speak.

"Look, I know this is hard, but anything you can give us would be appreciated."

I stare straight into her eyes and I hope she feels all the hatred in my gaze.

"I don't have anything I'd like to tell you," I sneer. I've had to talk to cops before. I never said a word. And I'm sure as hell not going to now.

Not when what I say would contribute to losing him forever.

"Did you know Tony Lewis?" she asks and I shake my head. Again not wanting to speak, but she waits for me to say it out loud. The pen in her hand pressed to the pad.

"Never met him."

"Do you know where your husband would go to acquire cocaine?"

My expression turns hard as I tell her, "My husband doesn't do coke." I want to add *anymore*. He's done it before. He told me. He's done a lot of shit that I'm ashamed of, but that was before me.

Detective Nicoli smirks at me and flips the page over in her notepad then says, "We'll have the warrant for a sample from him soon."

Absently my hand drifts to my stomach, to where our baby is growing, as if protecting this little one will protect Evan. But I'm quick to pull it back as one of the heavier bags slips forward on my arm.

She doesn't need to know, but I want to tell her. I want to tell the world my Evan could never do what they're saying he did. But I don't tell her a damn thing.

"Good for you," I tell her and start to walk past her again. I shove the key into the lock and turn it, but before I can open it, the cop leans against the door and waits for me to look at her.

"Get out of my way," I seethe, my anger coming through. Anger at Evan, anger at her.

"Someone's going down for Tony Lewis' death."

"Someone should, but my husband is not a murderer," I finally snap. I grip the handle tight, feeling the intricate designs in the hard metal press against my skin. It's freezing and the lack of circulation in my arms hurts. But I can't let go. I don't trust myself.

"I'm going inside and I have nothing left to say," I tell her and every word comes out with conviction.

"I'll leave my card," she says and slips it into one of the bags dangling from my arm.

I watch her walk away, not saying another word and biting back the comment on the tip of my tongue for her not to bother.

"Fucking bitch," I spit out the second I open the door and then let the bags fall to the floor.

My body feels like ice and my arms and shoulders are killing me. My legs are weak as I lean against the door to shut it and stare absently ahead, my gaze drifting from the empty foyer to the stairs.

I want to cry.

I want to give up.

But mostly I wish I'd been a better wife. I wish I'd kept Evan from whatever the hell he did.

I know him. He's not a murderer.

CHAPTER 3

Evan

Damaged, scarred and ruined,
My life all but destroyed.
Nothing but a gaping hole,
With revenge to fill the void.
I should have seen it coming,
But I was blinded by the lies.
And now I've succumbed to my sins,
With death to be my prize.

EVERY SECOND that ticks on that fucking clock makes me want to break it.

I haven't felt like this since the first time I was brought

into jail. It wasn't here; it was somewhere in Chicago. But this need to get the fuck out and handle all the hell I created is the exact same feeling I felt that first night.

Tick, the clock's minute hand moves again and I look to my right, staring down the woman at the front desk who's doing the paperwork for my release.

My neck cracks as I stretch out my shoulders. I haven't slept and I'm exhausted, but only pure adrenaline is pumping through my veins.

I need to get the hell out of here.

I knew something was off from the very beginning. James tried to fuck me over. It had to be him.

The only reason I can think of would be because of Samantha though, and that shit doesn't make sense. It's been years since we had that affair. Years for her husband to get over it. Shit, all he's been talking about for weeks is how he wants their divorce to be finalized.

I lean back on the metal bench and force myself not to look at the secretary and not to look at the clock either. My eyes focus on the corners of the cheap linoleum tiles and I drown out the sounds of the police station.

No noise, just the memory of that night coming back to me.

My shoulder flinches as I remember the feel of James' hand on my shoulder, showing me where the rec room in the hotel is and asking me if I need anything else. My eyes close and I can see him handing me the key card and looking to his left and right before telling me to make sure I show Tony a good time.

My lungs still and my vision turns red as my teeth grind against one another and my fists clench.

I can't fucking handle this. If that fucker set me up to die, he's a dead man.

And if it wasn't him, who was it?

"Mr. Thompson." A small voice to my right says my name and breaks my concentration. It takes every effort to raise my head up and relax my body as if nothing's wrong.

Each step smacks off the floor with the ticking of the clock. My heart beats in rhythm.

No one can know that I know. Not a soul.

"Your belongings," she says flatly. A weak smile forms on her thin lips as she hands me a Ziploc bag and tells me what each item is, going down the list in her hands.

It's all procedure, I tell myself.

I shove my hands into my pockets and rock on my heels

as I wait. Each second makes me more and more anxious to get out of here.

"And your keys," she says and then finally meets my eyes again.

"Thank you," I tell her and grab my shit. As I slip my black leather wallet into my back pocket, I wonder what James will say. Better yet, I wonder how I can get him to confess.

"Make sure you sign here," she says. I smile as I do what I'm supposed to.

Break his knuckles.

"And here," she adds, pointing to a line on the release forms.

Bash his knees in with a tire iron.

"You're all set, Mr. Thompson."

Put a gun to his head.

I force the left corner of my lips up as if I'm happy to be getting out of here. But my muscles are wound tight and my stomach's churning.

All because of one question: What if it wasn't him?

No one can know about any of this shit. My heart skips a beat and I hesitate to walk out of the station. *Kat.*

I force myself to move forward. I can't go to the cops, even to protect her. All they'll do is go after me. I don't have a shred of evidence. I have nothing but my word. And inside these four walls, my word doesn't mean shit.

The sky's gray as I glare through the glass doors, hating this place and what I've done. I have to tell her; I shake my head at the thought. I'll have to tell her I'm coming home first and with that thought I take out my phone. Pressing the power button to turn it on, I lean against the door waiting to see what I'm up against.

I bet she's heard I'm locked up, but maybe there's a small chance that she hasn't.

As the phone comes to life, a series of pings follows the messages popping up.

One from Pops, first asking where I am and if Kat forgave me. The next asking me to call him when I get out of jail. My heart sinks in my chest and the feeling of disappointment runs through me. He's too old to be dealing with my shit.

My body sags against the door, the cold from the autumn night seeping through the hard glass.

I scroll through the messages from people I don't give a shit about asking all sorts of questions. They don't matter.

But the one person who does matter, the only one I want to hear from and the only person I want to run to … not a single text.

I check the missed calls to make sure, although hopelessness runs through my veins. I swallow thickly and push the glass door open with a hard slam of my fists.

I hate that she didn't call me. That she didn't care enough to let me know that she heard. If Pops has heard, she's heard.

The bitter cold air whips by my face as I move toward the corner.

I check through my messages again, searching for her name like I could've missed it. One catches my eye. Samantha, James' wife. I pause over her name and read her text. *We need to talk.*

My strides become quicker at the thought of meeting up with her. She might know something. She might be my way to get what I need from James.

I have to go to Kat first and knowing that, I text Sam back, asking when and where.

I glance up at the corner, seeing the don't walk sign and take a look over my shoulder to hail a cab. I'm going home, whether Kat likes it or not.

I've kept so many secrets from her.

My head hangs low as I step out into the busy streets of New York City and a cab pulls up. The door slams shut with a loud click, dulling the city noises as I tell the driver our address. It's only after a few minutes of quiet, the rumble of the car almost lulling me to sleep, that I rub my tired eyes and think about what Kat would say. What she'd do if she knew the shit I got myself into.

She's already so close to hating me.

She's close to being over me and what we had.

I can't risk losing her, but right now either choice–to come clean, or to hide it from her–either choice feels like I've already lost her.

CHAPTER 4

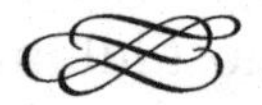

Kat

It's not in my nature to tempt you,
It's just that I'm so alone.
It's a darkness that's all-consuming,
Leaving me chilled to the bone.
Your smile makes me feel something,
To fill the hole my love left behind.
It's not my desire to lead you on,
But seduction isn't a crime.

"I JUST WANT to thank you for meeting me," Jacob says as my keys clink on the coffee shop table and I take a seat across from him.

It's been three days since Evan came back to the townhouse. And three days since he punched Jacob and accused me of cheating on him. Three days of me hiding away in our bedroom and pretending like this isn't my life.

But at some point I had to come out.

"I'm so sorry," I say with my eyes closed tight as I settle down into the seat. It's a wicker chair with a dark red cushion and the smell of coffee from the café adds to the comfort. The whole place has a homey feel to it.

My cheeks are practically frozen from the bitter wind whipping through West Village, but even still they burn.

"Don't," Jacob stops me, holding his hand up and waving off my embarrassment.

I can't believe how out of hand things have gotten. As a professional, I'm mortified. Who am I kidding? I haven't been professional with Jacob from the beginning.

"Please, Jacob." I shake my head slightly and then look up at him, staring into his eyes as I refuse to let him downplay everything. "What happened the other day was ridiculous. Evan had no right to put his hands on you, and firstly I want to thank you for not pressing charges."

"I don't blame him, Kat," Jacob says with an ease that catches me off guard. My heartbeat quickens and it's the only thing I can hear for a brief moment while I take in his words.

"It's fine, really. I mean it, I don't blame him."

I slowly take off my coat as I tell him, "I do. I know it looked a little off." A feeling of confusion clouds my memory of what I'd planned to say.

I was going to thank him for not pressing charges.

Beg him to not hold it against the publishing agency.

And concede that I would not be his contact if he did go with us. Obviously, I can't represent him after what happened. I'm prepared for that.

"He shouldn't have done it, and I feel awful."

"It wasn't you who did it," Jacob says.

The comfort in his voice makes me uneasy.

The next words out of his mouth add to that nervousness. "I'm kinda glad he did."

"Why?" I ask quietly.

"You two split, right?" Jacob asks.

"Yeah," I answer him and it makes my throat go dry. My chest feels hollow, nothing there but the raw emotion I'm trying to ignore.

“He’s not acting like it, judging by the way he talks to you. He’s aggressive. He’s doing what my ex did to me. And I don’t like it.”

“I don’t know what he’s thinking right now, but this isn’t him.”

“Either way, I knew I was pissing him off and I’m sorry. Again, I don’t blame him.”

I don’t know what to say back. There’s a tension between us that’s different from what I anticipated.

“I don’t like the way I saw him treat you,” Jacob says with a softened voice and then raises his hands up as if expecting retaliation from me. “I know I only saw a small piece. A sliver, even.” He licks his lower lip and then adds, “I just didn’t like it. So if he’s going to take it out on me instead, I’ll take it.”

“I wish you wouldn’t have done that,” I tell him honestly.

“I’m sorry. I really am. I knew it the second I walked down the stairs that I should’ve stayed out of it. It’s just something about what I see between you guys. It gets to me.”

“Between us?” I ask him.

“How you obviously care for him even though it’s killing

you," he says with a sadness in his eyes that could be a reflection of mine.

"Either way," he says, "I'm sorry and you don't have a reason to be."

"I didn't anticipate you being the one apologizing today."

Jacob shrugs and it's then that I see a faint bruise on his jaw. With the rough stubble, it almost blends in, but when I catch sight of it, I cringe.

"Shit," I say out loud and want to cover my face with my hands. Jacob smiles at me and a masculine chuckle makes his t-shirt tighten on his broad shoulders.

"Seriously, Kat," he says and moves his hand to the table, turning it slightly so it's palm up. "Don't worry about it. I can see where he's coming from."

Jacob's gaze flickers to a white mug on the table. I glance down at it; it's chai, and a warmth flows through me at the thought.

"So it's all okay?" I ask him.

He shrugs again and takes a sip from the mug. "If you're okay?" he finally answers and *okay* is not exactly the word I'd use to describe myself right now.

"For you, miss," a woman to my right announces, startling me and catching me by surprise. The barista I barely noticed when I first walked in sets down an identical mug to Jacob's in front of me. The spices of cinnamon and nutmeg hit me immediately and I welcome the scents.

"Thank you," I tell her although my eyes are on Jacob.

"I thought you'd like it," he says with a grin. "I know the shop is new, but I've had their chai almost every day and you have to try it," he says like we're good friends. Like we know each other well. After a moment he adds, "Great place to write."

"I could see that." I swallow, feeling a stir of something else in my chest. It pulls at my heart. *Guilt.* I feel like I'm cheating.

Evan and I are separated; I have to remind myself again. And with all the shit Evan's done, it's over. It has to be.

My hands wrap around the mug and they warm instantly as I take a look around the place. The brick walls and picture frames make it cozy and inviting. With the dark wooden tables and wicker chairs, I could see how a writer could make themselves comfy in a corner chair. I take a sip and then another, feeling the warmth flow through my cold chest. And then a third. Even though I feel less consumed with regret about the fight between Jacob and Evan, a different feeling is washing through me.

Like I'm to blame. And like Jacob's intentions for inviting me here have nothing to do with the fight or his work. I'm getting a good sense of what Jacob's intentions are.

"So what do you think?" Jacob asks me and I have to blink away my thoughts and try to figure out what he's referring to.

I think Jacob liked the fight. And I don't know why that doesn't infuriate me. That's what I think. The betrayal sinks slowly into my veins.

"The chai," he says and nods to my hands.

"It's good," I say with a halfhearted smile and then set it down. "Jacob, it wasn't okay what happened. And I really am sorry."

He forces a smile onto his lips and it's quiet for a short moment. "Kat, I don't really like your ex."

Ex.

My heart hammers and my blood feels as if it's draining from my body, leaving me cold. "I can see why," I tell him, although I can't look him in the eyes.

"Hey, I don't want to upset you." His voice changes to a tone that's sympathetic and I hate this moment. I hate feeling weak and not knowing what to do or say.

"Please don't worry about me, Jacob," I tell him as strongly as I can.

"First of all," he says with that gorgeous smile, "it's Jake." I can't help the small laugh that erupts from me at how serious he was when he said that. "And secondly, I'm not worrying, just being there for someone. That's all."

All my hesitations about him leave me as I look into his kind green eyes. He's the rugged kind of handsome I would have been drawn to back when I was single. I'm honest enough to admit I'm drawn to him now.

He's a good guy, and I can feel that in my bones.

"That's very nice of you, but I think," I start to say and try to figure out how to word what I'm thinking without sounding pathetic. *I'm still in love with my husband. Even if he's in jail ... and we're separated.* Instead, all I can manage is a mix between a groan and a sigh.

"Hey, let's just end it there?" he suggests. "I don't have many friends here and I put my nose where it didn't belong. I'm the one who's sorry."

"You're not in the wrong here," I tell him.

"I'm not in the right either, am I?" he asks.

"What do you mean?" I ask him, like I'm oblivious. I know exactly what he means.

"I-" he starts to say something but then he stops himself and lets out a short laugh before rubbing his eyes. "Sorry, I've been up all night working on this manuscript."

I take the moment to move back to work. To steer this relationship back to just business.

"And have you thought about who you'd like to be your agent and represent you?" Even I almost roll my eyes at the thought.

"You're shameless," he says with a wicked grin.

"I know," I answer him and smile into my cup. The smile is oddly genuine given my state just a moment ago, but Jacob has a way of making me feel calm and relaxed.

"I'm not ready to talk to any publishers. I still don't know what I want to do with this one yet."

"Want to tell me about it?" I ask him.

"Well, it's about me. Sort of." He leans back and spreads his legs wider, my eyes drawn down his chest as he runs his hand through his hair, looking out of the picture window at the front of the shop. "My ex, really."

I nod my head and reply, "So it's an emotional book for you. Maybe one to feed your soul, more than your family."

"Well I have no family to feed, so that'd be an easy one," he jokes. "But yeah. It's more just for me, I think."

"And what's it about, if you don't mind me asking?" I pry gently as I pick up a sugar packet on the table. I have no intention of adding it to my drink, but I think best when I have something to pick at. And I'm grateful for the distraction. I'd rather talk books all day long than anything else.

"We were high school sweethearts who beat the odds. But we just didn't get that happily ever after, you know?"

I feel a pang in my chest, a sharp pain in my heart; one that knocks the wind out of me. Another romance story gone wrong. "Why not?" I ask hesitantly.

"She'd been cheating on me for a while. Found out when she got pregnant and the dates didn't add up."

"That'll do it," I say as my mind wanders back to Evan. And his infidelity before we were married. And to my little secret.

"Turns out it was my best friend."

"Oh shit," I tell him and feel gutted for him. "Double betrayal."

"That'd make a good title," he says and then chews on his lower lip.

Again the feeling of shame settles on my shoulders. Evan and I are over, and I shouldn't feel like this is wrong. But for the first time in years, I feel *something* for someone else.

There's no way I can justify this feeling right now. Not when I haven't had a moment to get over Evan. Not when the thought of getting over him cripples me.

"You think I could sell it?" Jacob asks me. He holds my gaze as he lifts his cup.

"I'd have to see it first," I tell him even though I know a happily ever after sells better.

"Well, I'm still writing it. I think the story is still going well though," he says and every inch of my skin catches on fire. It's the way he looks at me. How his stare holds me captive. Or maybe it's the tone of his voice.

"Send me the first few chapters?" I ask him and then reach for my purse. "I have to get going, I'm sorry. I didn't think the meeting would last this long."

He half-smiles at me, a lazy smile almost as he says, "Okay then." He says it like he knows I'm lying, but more than that, like it amuses him. And again I question why that doesn't infuriate me.

Running isn't my style. I'm an approach things head-on kind of girl. But even I'm smart enough to know when

I'm set up to lose, and Jacob is only going to lead to more problems.

I start to take out my wallet to pay, but Jacob stops me. "Don't even think about paying."

"Are you sure?" I ask him and he's quick to answer.

"You can get the next one if you really want to, but this one is on me."

I give him a tight smile, although I'm grateful. Truly I am. Even if his intentions are less than pure.

I can only nod and then make my way out. It's all too much. Separation, pregnancy. Now Evan's in jail. I can't take how quickly my life is unraveling.

"Hey, Kat," Jake says from behind me as I push the door open and the bells ring. I turn to my left, and look back at him.

"It's going to be okay," he tells me and I say thanks although it's so softly spoken I don't think he could have possibly heard it.

I just have to leave. That's the only thing on my mind, because I'm so fucking broken that the words *it's going to be okay* are my undoing.

CHAPTER 5

Evan

Hidden in the shadows,
Are the secrets that tear me down.
They scratch and bite and rip apart,
Then leave me here to drown.
I'll protect you from them always,
Don't try to save me now.
The sins will come for you – they will,
The sins that broke my vow.

THE WORST SOUND in the world to me, is the sound of my wife crying.

And the worst sight I could ever imagine, is her bundled

into a ball on the kitchen floor, sobbing against the cabinets. Her shoulders heave as she lets out another sob and it makes me feel that much worse.

I didn't know it could get any lower than this.

"Kat," I say her name gently. She's crying so hard she didn't hear me come in. My voice startles her and she jumps back slightly, causing the cabinet door to shake behind her.

Her mouth falls open slightly, but she doesn't say anything. It looks like she's holding her breath.

"What's wrong?" I ask her and hate myself. It's fucking obvious. "What can I-"

"Nothing," she says shortly, cutting me off. "I'm fine." She uses the sleeve of her shirt to wipe her tears away, leaving her cheeks bright pink and tearstained.

"You aren't," I tell her.

"I'll be fine," she answers and her tone is harsher than usual. I suppose for good reason.

"I don't want to cry in front of you," she says with sincerity. Not to hurt me, just to tell me the truth as I walk deeper into the kitchen.

"That's what I'm here for," I tell her and then feel like an asshole. I haven't been here in days.

I can see Kat's lips part with some sarcastic response.

"I know we're going through shit and I'm not making things any better. But I'm here now." She doesn't respond as she pushes her hair out of her face.

I can't help but notice the curve of her shoulders and the way her breasts move as she steadies her breathing. My body is ringing with the need to touch her. The need to make her pain go away. "Whatever it is," I tell her, "it's going to be okay." I don't know how many nights I've told her that.

And it's always been true.

"I'm crying because of you!" she screams at me and brushes away her tears angrily.

"I'm sorry, babe. It's not what you think," I tell her, assuming this has to do with spending a night in jail. Fuck, I hope it's not something else.

She only huffs in disbelief and shakes her head, refusing to look at me. My blood turns cold and I struggle to move, to breathe, but still I walk toward her.

I can't lose her.

"Kat," I say her name and she doesn't look at me.

As I crouch down next to her, Kat gets up just to get away

from me and it kills me. Pushing up on her knee and then wiping under her eyes as she turns from me.

Her shoulders shudder as she opens a cabinet and reaches for a glass.

All I can hear is her heavy breathing as she tries to calm herself down.

"They broke in through the window," she says with a shaky voice and my blood goes cold.

"Who?" I ask and she shrugs her shoulders, looking at me with an expression of disbelief and answering sarcastically, "How the fuck should I know?"

"Where?" I ask her and follow as she walks to the guest bathroom. The second the door opens, I'm hit with the freezing air coming in through the broken window. It's only a powder room and inside the tub are shards of glass.

"They got in through the stairs on the back of the building. Didn't take anything that I can tell."

"What the fuck," I mutter beneath my breath, my fists clenching at my sides. "Were you home?" I ask her quickly. I should have been here. I should have been protecting her.

She shakes her head no. "I called the cops as soon as I got

in. I knew something was off. They went through your drawers, by the way. You may want to check to see if you had anything in there."

Fuck. My heart hammers as Kat leaves me to go back to the kitchen. I stand there numb with fear.

I don't know who it was or what they were looking for. But if she'd been here …

"Kat, please," I beg her, willing my legs to move and follow her back to the kitchen.

"I don't want to talk about it," she says without even looking at me.

"Kat, I need to know-" I start to say, but she cuts me off.

"If you want to talk, then tell me how jail was. How about that?" she spits back.

"Don't please me, don't touch me, don't anything me," she says, glaring over her shoulders as she slams the cabinet door. Her eyes are red-rimmed and she looks paler than usual.

She fills the glass with water and drinks down half of it with her back to me.

I want to reach out and hold her, but I've never seen her like this.

"Kat, I can explain."

"Oh, thank goodness. I was worried for a minute," she says and her voice drips with sarcasm, her back still to me as she turns the tap back on and fills the glass again.

"Please, if you don't mind, you could start with ... I don't know," she shrugs and turns to face me, the bitterness in her voice never more apparent than now. "Why I should give a damn about whatever excuse you have?"

My brow furrows as I take in her stance. She slams the glass down and waits. Her hair falls in front of her face, hiding part of her tired eyes and she doesn't bother to push it away.

"I don't want you to be mad," I start to say but then take her in.

Her knuckles turn white as she grips the counter and I know right then, I can't tell her what I think about James. I can't tell her that I think someone was trying to kill me or that I'm bringing more trouble to her.

I have to be the man she *wants* me to be.

I can do that. Just one more lie. Just once more.

I swear it'll be the last. And only so I can hold on to her.

"Kat, I don't know a thing about the coke or James or whatever the hell anyone's told you."

"You said you needed an alibi," Kat says straightfaced. She blows part of the hair away from her face and then crosses her arms across her chest.

My stomach sinks as I give her just a little. Just enough. "This is why. I knew Tony was dead, but I wasn't involved." *Lie.* I can barely stand on my own two feet knowing I just lied to her.

"Why an alibi?" she asks.

"To save the company's image. We couldn't be associated with it any more than we already were." It's only a thinly veiled lie. It's mostly true.

Kat nods her head, putting a finger to her lips and letting the words sink in as she stares at the floor.

"So you gave him the coke?" she asks and her eyes flash to mine.

"No," I tell her and my voice is hard. "I told you I don't do that shit." *Lie. Another lie.* I'm digging my hole deeper.

"They're going to test you," Kat says like she doesn't believe me.

"I'll have them show you the results if and when they do," I say and my words come out bitter.

She turns her back to me again and I walk closer to her as she fills the glass with more water.

"I mean it. I promise you. It was just a job and I barely drank, Kat."

She doesn't look at me as I come closer, close enough to touch her, but I don't.

"I did drink, but that's it. I swear to you. I wouldn't touch that shit."

She sets the glass down and then looks at me as she says, "Tony did."

She walks past me, brushing her shoulder against mine.

"I quit for a reason," I tell Kat, begging her to listen and to forgive me. "I didn't do anything, and if anyone in the world would believe me, it would be you." My voice shatters on the last word and I have to swallow my plea.

"I believe you," Kat says instantly, hating that she's causing me pain. This is why she's too good for me, but I'll be damned if I don't do everything I can to keep her.

"No secrets?" she asks me and there's a change in her expression.

I shake my head no, although I feel like a fucking coward.

"I have one," she tells me softly.

"What's that?" I ask her, sending the air changing between us, darkening and chilling.

"I have a doctor's appointment tomorrow," she tells me and her eyes flicker to me and then anywhere else. She can't look at me and the sense that she's hiding something from me takes over.

"The doctor's? You alright?" I ask her, my voice low. I take one step closer to her and wait for her to move back, but she doesn't.

She shrugs and stares at the countertop.

"What's going on, Kat?" I ask her, listening to my heart beat hard and then harder as she makes me wait.

Her forehead scrunches the way it does just before she cries and I chance another step closer to her. I can feel the heat from her body as she sniffles and then looks away from me.

"It's okay," I whisper. I reach out for her, praying she lets me hold her and she does.

"Baby, it's okay," I tell her as I pull her small body into my arms. God, I needed this. I hold her as close as I can, rocking her slightly and loving how she grips onto me right back. Her shoulders are stiff at first, but she gives in and I say a silent prayer thanking God for it.

I hold her like I have for years, and it feels so natural. So right.

"Just tell me what it is, sweetheart," I whisper in her hair as she sobs into my chest. It hurts. Every bit of her sadness shreds me. "I'm sorry," I tell her and then pull back to look at her, but she just buries her face back into my chest.

It's a long moment before Kat quietly pulls away.

"I have something you should see," she says and starts walking off. She wraps her arms around her torso as I follow her toward the stairs.

Anxiety suffocates me, not knowing what it is she wants to show me.

"Stay here," she tells me, looking over my shoulder as she grips the railing.

I nod and watch her walk. Slow steps. Her feet pad against the floor as she leaves me.

I wait with bated breath. My body begs me to sit down, the exhaustion making me want to give in and fall into the couch. But I stand and wait.

Whatever it is, a picture of some shit I did, a text or a letter–I don't care what it is that's making her so damn upset. I'll fix it.

I won't let her go and I'll destroy anyone and everyone who gets between us.

My head lifts when I see her come down the stairs and my feet move of their own accord.

They don't move for long though. The second my eyes land on the white plastic stick in her hands, my body freezes.

My mouth hangs open just slightly as I glance from the pregnancy test to Kat's face.

She stops in front of me, barely looking at me and holds it out. "I'm sorry," she whispers in a cracked voice. As if this is bad. As if she's done something wrong.

"Baby, why are you sorry?" I ask as I look between her and the stick. I can't will myself to take it or to even believe it's real. "You're pregnant?" I ask her. As she covers her mouth with her hand and nods, I can't for the life of me understand why she's so upset.

A baby. A little life just like my Kat.

It's the best damn thing I could have ever asked for.

And then it hits me. *Jacob Scott.* My breathing picks up as my blood heats. I don't have the nerve to ask her, but the words are on the tip of my tongue.

I'll kill him.

"I'm pregnant," Kat says and takes in a steadying breath, taking a few steps backward.

I almost ask her. But I can't do it. Even if the baby isn't mine, I don't care. I'll take care of both Kat and her child.

"A baby?"

"Yeah, a baby," she says and chances a look up at me. Her long, dark lashes glisten with what's left of the tears before she wipes them away.

"That's wonderful," I tell her and close the space between us, reaching for her hands. She leans into me and I rub the pads of my thumbs against her knuckles. "Kat," I swallow before asking, "why are you sorry about something so amazing?"

I can see her expression fall as she tries to stay strong.

"It doesn't change what's going on, but I just found out and I don't know."

"Don't know what?"

"How we're going to handle all of this," she says and starts to pull away from me.

"Kat, you're mine," I tell her as I pull her back to me.

"You were just in jail hours ago. How are you going to take care of your baby?"

"I'll be the best damn father I can be."

"You said that about being a husband too and we're separated-"

"And we're going to be fine," I say, cutting her off. "Better than fine. We're having a baby."

I finally look at her stomach. I wrap one of my hands around her hip and the other lays against Kat's stomach.

"I love you, and that's what matters."

"It's not the only thing that matters," she tells me back.

Her green eyes swirl with so much emotion, I can't stand it. "I'm telling you right now, Kat. Me loving you, it's the only thing that matters."

CHAPTER 6

Kat

Lost and confused,
There's nowhere left to hide.
The truth is I'm ruined,
That truth can't be denied.

Legs shaking, knees weak,
I've been his for far too long.
If I leave him, then who am I?
No, that must be wrong.

I need his touch; I need his lips,
The soft desire that does burn.
He's wrong for me, he'll hurt me,
But it's a love I can't unlearn.

I DON'T KNOW what to think or do.

I don't know what's right and wrong.

But I'm so aware of how I feel.

Every inch of skin burns with need against Evan's touch. He's got a spell over me. It must be some kind of dark magic, because he makes me forget reason. He makes me forget how angry I am at him.

I melt into him as if I was meant to be held by him from the very start.

The worst part is that I don't want him to ever let me go. Because the second he does, I'll remember. Time will resume and the moment will be ruined.

One of these times, I'm going to let him go and never be held again. I can feel it down in my very soul.

His hot breath tickles my neck as he whispers, "I love you, Kat."

And my soul quiets, the pain soothed. And for the moment, I grip on to him just as tightly as he holds me.

My heart clenches in my chest as I swallow the lump in my throat.

"I'm so happy," he barely breathes as he brushes his hand against my belly. "We're going to have a baby," he says reverently.

How can I not fall back to him when I know he loves me? How can I not cling to him, when he talks to me like this?

Every reason comes to me one by one, the truth too real to ignore.

My nails dig into his shirt as I push away from him. "We need to talk." I push the words out as he reluctantly watches me move away.

"If we do this, we're moving forward together?" I ask him.

He nods and says, "I promise."

"I just want to be with you, Evan." I speak from the bottom of my heart and I know it's the bottom because it's all I have left.

"I promise," he says again but his eyes are glossy.

"I'm sorry I wasn't the man I should have been for you," he says then grabs my hand and kisses my knuckles one by one before turning it over to kiss my wrist. "I'm sorry I fucked things up so bad." He looks away from me and I can't stand the look in his eyes.

"It's okay," I tell him, desperate to take the hurt away from his expression.

"I love you, and that's what matters," he tells me again. "Don't stop loving me. Please. No matter what happens," he begs me.

"You didn't do anything," I tell him. "Nothing will happen."

He looks me in the eyes and says, "Nothing will ever happen to you or this baby. I swear, Kat."

"Our baby," I whisper and put his hand on my belly. He lowers his head and I swear I think he's crying, but when he looks up at me he says, "Nothing will ever happen to you or our baby. I'll never put you in harm's way, Kat." He takes a deep breath.

"Just don't stop loving me," he says, almost like a plea.

"Don't stop loving me," I tell him back and he says beneath his breath, "It's all for you. I won't let anyone hurt you."

"Evan," I start as I reach for his jaw, feeling the intensity of his words and the chill that comes with it. But as my lips part, a startled yelp comes up. Evan's strong arms wrap around my waist and bring me to his chest as he carries me up the steps.

He sets me down gently on the bed, which is so at odds with how he kisses me. It's ravenous and reckless even. Desire scorches my skin and makes me scissor my legs.

He groans into my mouth as his hands slip between my thighs and under my panties and he runs his fingers up and down my pussy.

"So fucking wet," he groans with lust. "I love how you're always wet for me."

"Always," I repeat his word, but my head feels dizzy and the need for him to be inside of me overrides any sort of logic or reason.

I claw at his shirt, desperate to get it off and it makes him chuckle, a deep, low sound.

My eyes feel heavy as I open them to scold him for taking so long and leaving me wanting, but the words stay put in my throat as I watch him pull his shirt over his shoulders, revealing his tanned, tattooed skin and muscular physique.

I lick my lips with the need to kiss him and he grants me exactly that. Bracing one forearm by my head, he leans down to kiss me, pressing his lush lips against mine and tasting me with swift strokes. He pulls back to trap my bottom lip between his teeth as he pushes his jeans down.

It's a short, sharp pain that spikes through my body,

directly connected to my clit. When I open my eyes, letting the sweet gasp of longing escape, I'm lost in his gaze. Trapped under his dark hazel eyes and waiting for him. I'd do anything for him. I swear there's no way I could love him more in this moment.

"Evan, please," I start to plead with him not to leave me again. Not to make me choose between a life without him or a life without shame, but he cuts me off, mistaking my plea for what my body feels and not my heart.

"Spread your legs for me." He gives me the command and my body obeys before I can even fully register his words.

Every thrust is slow and deep. The air between our lips heats until I arch my neck with a moan, feeling his thick cock push deep inside of me, wanting more of me than I can give.

"Evan," I say his name reverently as my hardened nipples brush against his chest and he groans into my neck, holding himself inside of me.

"I love you," he whispers and then pulls out slowly. My body relaxes thinking he's keeping a slow pace, pulling himself nearly all the way out before pushing back in until he's buried to the hilt. But instead he slams himself into me and I scream out, my nails digging into his muscular shoulders as pleasure races through me.

"I'll never stop loving you," he says as he pounds into me again, his hips crashing against mine.

"Evan," his name slips from between my lips as my head presses against the pillow and thrashes from side to side. It feels too intense. Way too much for so soon. My breathing picks up as my toes curl and my legs wrap around his hips.

He rocks himself against me, his pubic hair brushing against my throbbing clit and I writhe under him, feeling my skin prick slowly with the need for just a little more. I can hardly breathe. "Evan," I moan and again it comes out as a strangled plea.

"Kat," Evan says and then nips my earlobe, sending a shudder across my body. "Never forget, that I would do anything for you. Everything for you."

CHAPTER 7

Evan

It's all for her, the thought rings clear,
It's all for her, my love, my dear.
I won't give up or let harm come,
I'll fight it all until I'm numb.
And even then, I'll protect her still,
Because, for her, I would kill.

It feels colder than usual as I walk down the sidewalk. It's empty, not a soul in sight. Not even down the alleyways and in the dark shadows. Someone's always there. Always watching and waiting.

But not tonight.

My boots crunch the light snow beneath my feet and fog fills my vision with each step I take to get home.

The light outside the townhouse flickers and catches my attention.

The silent night and darkness set in just as I walk up the stairs and open the door.

It's so quiet and my first thought is that I'm grateful she isn't crying anymore. Ever since I told her the truth, Kat hasn't been the same.

She looks at me the way I've always looked at myself. She's always sad now, with red-rimmed eyes and an expression of shame, and it's all because of me. I ruined her like I knew I would.

I call out to her in the townhouse. It's the same as it's always been, but there's an emptiness to it. A feeling that emanates from the white walls down into my bones.

"Kat!" I call out again, and my voice echoes from the kitchen.

My boots crunch although there is no snow.

My breathing picks up and again fog clouds my vision as I walk toward the kitchen. "Kat," I say her name but I already know she can't hear me.

The white mist fades and I see her. Just as she was yesterday, balled up on the floor, but she's not crying anymore.

Crimson red has seeped into her clothes.

"Kat," her name slips from me in disbelief as tears flow freely and I run to her.

"No!" I scream as her limp body falls on the floor and her eyes stare back at me, lifeless, but still red-rimmed.

A note falls from nowhere as I cradle her, rocking her and screaming for it not to be true. Praying for God to take it back. It flutters to the floor with an elegance I hate in this moment. I can't let go of Kat; I grip her tighter, reading the words as the ink on the paper appears slowly. The script is feminine and delicate.

You should have let me go. You should have protected me.

It's all your fault.

And then I hear a baby scream.

MY EYES SHOOT OPEN. My body's stiff and hot as my heart races, pounding in my chest like a war drum. Heavy, hard and unforgiving. *It's just a nightmare.*

"Kat," I whisper her name and move suddenly, shaking the bed as I put my arm around her.

It's the soft moan from her sleep that keeps me from shaking her.

My heart still pounds in my chest as she breathes easily beside me.

As if nothing's wrong. Like nothing's happened.

I blink away the sleep and terror as the early morning light streams into the room and the city traffic drowns out the gentle and steady sounds of Kat's breathing.

My body's heavy as I lie back into the bed, wiping the sweat from my brow and trying to forget the look on her face as I held her in my arms in the nightmare.

It's hard to swallow, and the fear is nearly crippling.

It's not real, I whisper. But I know with everything in me it's so much more.

Time ticks by slowly, and sleep doesn't come again for me.

I didn't lie just once last night. I lied twice.

The need to be with her made me do it. The need to hold on to her love and let her feel how much I love her. I had to take her pain away. But that makes today that much harder.

There are only two truths I know.

Someone's trying to kill me and if they can't get me, they'll come for her.

But only if they know we're still together. And right now, no one does.

I love Kat too much.

I almost leave a note after going through my dresser drawer, knowing there was nothing in there to take, but making sure nothing was left behind. The first thing I'm doing is having a security system installed. This shit won't happen again and that's how I was going to start the note.

I wanted to write one for Kat to say goodbye and that I'll be back then leave before she wakes.

But she deserves to at least know why I'm leaving. Only for a little while. Only until I know she's safe.

"THE DOCTOR'S appointment is at one I think," Kat says sleepily and I turn, my body stiff, to face her slowly. My eyes burn from the lack of sleep, but I don't care.

I welcome the pain.

"You're finally awake," I answer her and prepare myself for what I have to do.

The world thinks we've broken up. And it has to stay that way.

"You've been up long?" she asks me and yawns.

"Kat," I say her name and swallow my words.

I've been thinking about them all morning, the images of the nightmare feeling more and more real. And every possibility for what could happen running on a loop in my mind.

"I have to tell you something," I tell her as I stare at the dresser across the room. I look in the mirror but I can't see our reflection, only the closed door to the bedroom.

"It's only for a short time, but I have to go do something."

"What do you mean?" she asks and then sits upright. She reaches out for me, her soft, small hand gripping on to my shoulder so she can have my attention.

"I mean, I don't think I can go to the appointment today."

Her expression falls and she visibly retreats, pulling her knees up to her chest and wrapping the blanket tightly around her.

"Why not?" she asks with a little heat in her words. With every second that passes, I can see her getting angrier. "What's more important?"

"I don't think we should be seen in public together," I tell her and swallow the painful lump in my throat. No one knows we're together or that she's pregnant. "This has to stay a secret."

"Are you serious?" she asks me.

"Kat, I have to take care of some things."

"Bullshit! You don't have to do it! What about us? Our baby," she says and her voice cracks. "What about taking care of us?"

"I am," I tell her and my words come out strangled, shattering the delicate balance that was here only a moment ago.

"If you walk through that door, you're not coming back." Kat's voice shakes as she points a finger at me. Her eyes are wide and the grief I feel is reflected in them. "You can't keep doing this to me. I can't keep … " she trails off and hiccups, on the verge of tears.

"It's only for a short while," I tell her to reassure her.

"I don't understand." Kat shakes her head as if she thinks I'm crazy. As if what I'm saying is incomprehensible and maybe it is, but it's okay. The less she knows, the safer she is. And that's the only thing that matters.

"I have something I have to finish."

"You need to stop this, Evan. Please. I'm ready to move forward. We have a baby coming. We can do this, but you can't keep going backward."

God I wish she knew.

I could try to outrun it, but not with her by my side. I'll fight it and come back to her. I just need her to have faith. And I know she will. The last thought is what moves me to put space between us.

"Just believe me when I say I love you, but I can't be with you right now."

"Stop it! Stop it, Evan. Please! I don't care what it is, just leave it behind and stay with me. Please, I'm begging you."

"I'm so sorry," I tell her and hate that I'm causing her pain.

"Why are you doing this?" she whispers. "I can't believe … I can't … "

"I love you, Kat, but I can't do this right now." The words come out as if I'm ending it with her and that's when I realize it's what I have to do.

To protect her and my baby.

"I swear to God, if you walk out of that door, Evan, it's

over. I'm done playing games. You're here or you're not." Her words are restrained as she says them, each one looking more and more painful.

My chest tightens with an unbearable sorrow as I whisper, "I'm sorry, Kat."

CHAPTER 8

Kat

I'm worth something, that I know,
But that's not what I feel.
I should be strong and move on,
I think I need to heal.
Time has taught me to trust,
To have faith and to forgive.
Time is nothing but betrayal,
And lies are addictive.

WINTER HAPPENED OVERNIGHT. And it's a bitter one at that.

My hands are still freezing as I stare at the fire in Jules' great room. It's been painted and decorated since I was here only a week or so ago. Jules didn't waste any time making the space feel cozy and warm. The soft gray walls complement the cream furniture and stone fireplace perfectly.

"I love the color," I tell her in an attempt to cheer myself up and break the awkwardness in the room. Usually when we get together it's nothing but laughter.

"It's called Mineral Ice," Jules says agreeably from her spot on the chenille rug. Her glass of wine hasn't moved from the coffee table since I've walked in. Come to think of it, neither Maddie or Sue are drinking either.

The only one who seems normal is Maddie, and it's because she's lost her mind. I only just texted them days ago with the news that I'm pregnant and she's taken it upon herself to start planning every detail of the next nine months for me. I love her and the distraction, but there's no way I can even think about a baby shower right now.

"I think the grays and yellows will be perfect for a neutral theme," Maddie says. "We could do bees or elephants and it will all match this room perfectly."

Maddie has a few bags on the floor next to her. Each from different party shops with samples of all sorts of baby shower accessories and décor. She said it was a "few" things to look at in the group message.

I'd started a group message to vent to them about what had happened. Within two hours both Sue and Jules were at my side, pulling me together. It was Maddie's idea to meet up today and thank God they dragged me here. I'd rather be looking at tiny yellow clothespins and paper samples for invitations than hysterically crying on the floor in my bedroom. So I suppose this is a win.

"Thank you for offering to host it, Jules," I tell her, giving her a warm smile and feeling so damn ungrateful. All of this is so out of place with how I feel.

I'm just not happy, and I can't fake it. There's a hole in my chest and it feels like there's no way it could ever heal.

The father of my baby left me. Not just left me, but left me again, talking like a crazy person. He's lost it. That's what it really is.

I thought we were whole again last night; I felt it. Everything in me felt the love between us. And yet, this morning he walked away.

"Okay, so menu … " Maddie says, leaning over the laptop that's on the glass coffee table and clicking the keys.

"Isn't it a little early to start planning all this?" I ask them. "I can't be more than two months along at most."

Maddie stops whatever she's doing and looks up at me. "I just thought maybe it would be a way to cheer you up a bit?" she offers before sitting down on her butt, right next to Jules. They're closer to the fire sitting on the rug, but I'd rather be on the sofa.

"I don't think there's anything that's going to do that," I tell them woefully. My hand drifts to my midsection, but there's not even a tiny bump. There's no way I'd know I was pregnant if I wasn't peeing on a stick every other day to prove that it's real.

"Do you … want to … " Maddie struggles to suggest something else.

"Do you want to talk about what's going on?" Sue asks finally.

"I'm feeling so fucked up that I'm actually considering starting to write letters again," I confess to them and remember how I used to write to my mother when she died. It was what my therapist had suggested. "That's how low I feel," I tell them, emphasizing each word.

"You can tell us, you know?" Sue offers.

"I'll probably cry," I tell her with a sad smile and huff a sarcastic laugh. "I just wish someone could explain it. I feel crazy."

"Okay, so let's have the complete update," Jules says and squares her shoulders to give me her full attention.

"It's over." The words come out easier than I thought they would. Maybe I'm just numb to them, I don't know.

"For real?" Maddie asks me.

"Yeah, I'm not," I pause and shake my head and close my eyes. "I'm not doing this back and forth. I know where I want my life to go, I know what I need to do and Evan just isn't there."

"Did you tell him you're pregnant?" Sue asks me cautiously.

"Yeah," I tell them and swallow the pain that threatens me. "I told him and he was so happy." I have to put my hand up to my mouth to keep from getting emotional again.

"I think it's okay if you cry," Sue says. "You're going through so much and you can always blame it on hormones."

A soft, but genuine laugh sneaks in, shutting down the overwhelming heartache.

"I told him, and he still chose to leave."

"Why?"

"He didn't say," I tell them and then correct myself. "No wait, he did. He said," I try to quote him although I'm not sure if it's exact, "'I have to fix something I can't outrun, but it's only for a short while.'"

"What the fuck does that mean?" Maddie asks with her face scrunched up.

"I don't know!" I raise my voice in exasperation and that's exactly how I feel.

"Maybe he's worried about the stress from everything he's going through getting to you?" Sue offers and I stare daggers at her.

"As if leaving me is any better?" I practically snap at her.

Her hands fly into the air defensively as she says, "I take it back. He's such an asshole."

"He's not an asshole," I tell her but my words lose conviction as they come out.

"Here's your tea, sweetheart," Jules says and sits next to me on the plush sofa. The seat sinks in slowly, dipping as she gets comfortable beside me.

"I'm still so happy you're pregnant," Maddie says and reaches for my hand, squeezing it gently. "You're going to be the best mom," she says with such certainty even though she looks so sad.

"Do you want someone to come to the doctor's appointment with you?" Sue asks, but I shake my head.

"I'll be fine," I answer her.

"It's not about being fine, love," Sue says. "I could take pictures or something."

"Of her hooha?" Maddie jokes and Sue rolls her eyes.

"Just to have someone there," Sue suggests.

"I would love to go," Jules says.

"I just had one yesterday, so maybe next time." I feel like a liar using the appointment as an excuse.

"But you missed that one," Jules pipes up and reminds me of the truth. "You didn't go when Evan ... " Jules trails off, but "left" is the word she's looking for. Evan left me. I skipped my appointment and cried alone in bed instead.

"I didn't reschedule since I have to go again in a few weeks," I say, shrugging it off like it doesn't matter. Like I'm not worried that my baby can feel my pain. And that every night I cry alone in our bed I'm damaging this tiny life.

Like I'm already a horrible mother and all this shit is going to hurt my baby.

"I just want to get my life together," I say and take in a

calming breath. "I know what I want, and I'm going to go for it whether or not Evan is beside me."

"You deserve happiness," Maddie says and the other girls nod.

"I just wish Evan would stop living like he's twenty-one. And doing stupid shit."

"I can't imagine him walking away when he knows you're pregnant," Sue says although I'm not sure it was intended for me. She stares absently at the roaring fire, the crackling filling the silence that follows her words.

"I think that's what hurts the most. It was so ... when I told him, he was just so ... " I have to pause and close my eyes. I remember the way he held me and kissed me, and it kills me.

"Hey, now," Sue pipes up. "You're going to be fine regardless. He's got a situation he's dealing with."

I roll my eyes at the word "situation."

"The fact that he has any *situation* is the problem." All of my frustration flies out of my mouth. "We should have our lives together. Stability and a family."

It's silent once I've finished. Maddie looks down at the rug and Jules has an expression of sympathy although neither says anything.

"I agree," Sue says gently.

"It's going to be okay," Maddie speaks up although she doesn't look at me, she just picks at the rug. She shrugs and says, "Being pregnant and single is like the new trend anyway."

I let out a little laugh, and that breaks up the tension. Maddie even smiles.

"Well at least it's fashionable then." My hand moves to my belly subconsciously and a surge of strength eases my pain.

I can do this, and I deserve happiness. I'm worthy of that. If Evan doesn't think so, then he'll have to deal with the consequences.

"Fuck him," I tell them. "If he wants to keep this shit up, then he can do it alone."

I move the pillow on my right to my lap and hold on to it.

"You're going to be fine regardless," Sue repeats her earlier sentiment, the only one to speak.

I nod my head, but that's not how I feel.

"And we're going to throw you the best shower ever," Maddie says, interrupting my dark thoughts.

"What theme do you want? The elephants or bees … or

whatever else is in that bag?" Jules asks me as if it's all we should be talking about. And I suppose it is. I'm done with Evan and his bullshit.

"I'll have to think about it," I tell her and bury myself into the sofa. A light feeling seems to lift my shoulders, like a weight is gone. Maybe it's the feeling you get when you're truly done with someone. When there's no way they can make it right again and you've come to accept it.

Maddie starts talking about baby showers, and her voice is peppy as she pulls out an iPad from her bag and says something about a Pinterest board.

My gaze falls on each of the girls, all of them here for me. Jules catches my eye and rests her hand on my thigh, mouthing the words, "It's going to be okay."

And for a short moment, maybe a second or two, I feel like it might.

Evan needs time to realize what it means to be the man I need.

Hopefully the time I need to get over him completely and stop falling for his charm is less than that. Because I can't do this again. I can't and I won't.

UNTITLED

Diary Entry 1

Mom,

It's been a while.

I miss you guys, but you already know that. I could really use your advice now.

I know Evan loves me. I can feel it when he looks at me, but when he's not with me, I feel like he doesn't. I know I'm insecure, but he's been so weird lately. He's acting crazy and it scares me.

I don't even want to tell you. I'm so ashamed.

It's that bad.

I know you never met him, but I swear he's a good guy. I know he is.

But the thing is, he's not doing good things.

And the worst part is that he's not stopping.

He knows we're pregnant, and he's not stopping. It doesn't get much worse than that, does it?

I don't know what to do.

He wants me to just wait for him and I love him so much.

But I'm scared, Mom.

I'm scared he doesn't really love me and that this is all going to hurt the baby.

I cry all the time. And that can't be good for our little one.

I remember you crying when I was little and how you held me and sang lullabies to me. I'm trying that late at night. I hold my belly and try to sing lullabies instead of crying. I'm trying so hard, but I'm afraid I'm already failing.

I don't think I can be with someone who isn't willing to stop doing what he knows is wrong. It's not just me anymore.

But it gets worse.

I can’t stop loving him. I don’t know what’s wrong with me, Mom. I could use your lullabies right now.

CHAPTER 9

Evan

Threats can make you weak,
To think of what's to come.
To avoid seeing what's here and now,
And live life as if you're numb.
The lies are threading webs,
To trap and hold you still.
The sinners that hide in plain sight,
Hold your fate against your will.

New York City is a sight to be seen. It's the nightlife, the skyscrapers, the people themselves. But winter is when it's the most beautiful, I think.

Only the trees are wrapped with Christmas lights this early in November, but soon everything will be covered in white and blue lights. The windows will be decorated on all of the shops in Rockefeller Center and people will come from around the world to see it.

It's stunning, but what's best about it, is that it's crowded. During the winter months, this block is constantly packed. And that's exactly what I need right now.

I have to take off one of my gloves to turn my phone on and check the messages. My foot taps on the hard cobblestone beneath my feet as I wait on an iron bench.

The phone goes off in my hand and I stare at the message from my father.

Just a bit overworked because of my dumbass son.

Are you sure you're alright? I ask him and ignore the insult.

It's fine.

If you went to the hospital, I text, *it must've been bad.* On the subway here I got the message from my father that he was being released. He said he felt lightheaded in the grocery store and the manager called him an ambulance. He said they were just being dramatic, but I know my father. He's stubborn and hates hospitals.

I'm fine. Go make it right with your wife, he tells me and I have to tear my eyes away from the phone.

I'm trying.

I hesitate to tell him, but the cold sickness flowing through my veins begs me to text my father, *She's pregnant.* I can't help it. I'm so fucking proud. Like I did something amazing for the first time in my life.

His response is immediate.

Thank God. Now she has to forgive you right? he texts back and I let a small chuckle escape.

I wish it were that easy. *That's not how it works, Pops,* I tell him.

He messages back, *It's Pop-Pop now. I'm so happy for you two.*

Fuck, it shreds me to even think about telling him the truth, so I don't.

My phone pings again and this time it's not my father, it's the person I've been waiting for. *I'm here.*

A few children shriek in laughter as they run by me and I lift my eyes up, watching them chase each other. And that's when I see her.

Samantha.

I shove the phone in my pocket, standing up and putting my glove back on and shoving my hands into my pockets as I walk toward her.

"Thank you for meeting me," Sam says with bright red cheeks that match the tip of her nose. Her hair's been blown by the wind around her face, although she has on a white beanie and a coordinating scarf and gloves. She slips her phone into her black wool jacket and says, "I feel like I'm being paranoid."

"Tell me what's going on."

"James messaged me and said what happened to Tony could happen to me and to lay off the demands for the divorce."

"As in ... an overdose."

"I don't know." She takes a deep breath and looks to her left and right as her face crumples. "I think just ... I think he was threatening to kill me."

"Are you okay?" I ask her and she shakes her head. Fuck, it shreds me to see her like this. I won't let him get away with this.

"The coke was laced with poison and the cops are convinced it was intentional," I tell her.

"I would say I don't think James is capable of that," Sam

says with sad eyes. As she breathes, her breath turns to fog. "But he's done things before … "

"Things like what?" I ask her.

"He's choked me, thrown me against the wall. He's threatened me before. But he's never … " Her eyes get glossy as she says, "I didn't think he would ever do it."

"You think he killed Tony?"

She nods her head once, a frown marring her face as she gets choked up. "He said it was for you," she speaks softly, her eyes flickering from me to the cars driving behind us.

I don't give her a response in the least, hiding the anger as my heart thuds hard in my chest at the confirmation of what I already knew.

"What did I do?" I ask her.

"It's because of me," she says and her voice cracks.

"You didn't do this."

"You don't understand," she says, gaining more composure and wiping under her eyes as the wind whips between us and forces her hair behind her. "He wants me to give him everything in the divorce. The properties, the business, he's not budging."

"I thought it was finalized?" I ask her.

She shakes her head and says, “I pushed back.” Her words come out hard. “He’s pushed me around for so long and he thought he could just get rid of me and throw me away like he did his first wife. But I made this business.”

“So he went after me?”

“To prove a point.”

“And what’s that?” I ask her.

“That he could eliminate whoever he wants.”

Anger narrows my gaze as I tell her, “He missed his shot.”

“He’ll do it again,” she tells me, “and I’m scared.”

“It’ll be alright,” I tell her although I’m not sure it will be. I’m already trying to figure out how to end this. How to put that asshole nine feet in the ground.

“Please help me, Evan,” she begs and her voice is coated in agony. “I don’t know where to go or what to do.”

“The police,” I tell her and it’s the first time in my life I’ve ever thought of going to them. “You can tell them everything.”

“He has them in his back pocket,” she says bitterly and then adds, “You know that. Did they tell you anything?”

I shake my head no and say, “Only that the coke was laced to kill. It was made into a murder weapon.”

"Oh, God," Samantha lets out a gasp and hunches forward slightly. I feel the need to put my arm out to steady her and she clings to me.

A moment passes in the wintry cold where I think back to a few times we've gotten out of tight spaces. I thought a client here and there would go to trial, but they never did. I didn't think it was because of James though. I thought they didn't have enough evidence.

"He'll go down for what he did," I tell her as one name and one face come to mind. Mason. Jules' husband. He's gotten off for murder, just last month.

He killed his father and everyone knows it.

He's from a different world than me, but I know him from back in the day when the rich kid was pissed and wanted to cut loose. I don't have a thing against him although I haven't spoken to him since I split up a fight a few months ago.

He owes me for that. And Mason's the type of man who pays his dues.

"What are you going to do?" she asks me. She scoots closer to me, almost too close, and I take a step back.

"I know a guy," I tell her and she's quick to nod but then her face falls.

"Fuck," she whispers, her eyes focused behind me and I whip my head around to see what she's looking at.

"It was him," she says and then covers her mouth. "Shit," she says with tears in her eyes.

"He can't hurt you," I tell her, turning around and keeping an arm behind me to protect her. My eyes search the crowd but I don't see him.

Her hands tug at my arm, pulling me back to her. Her bright red lips glisten as she licks them and tells me, "He went down to the subway, but he saw us. I know he did. At least I think he did," she says then closes her eyes tight and takes a step back. "It was definitely him."

"Is he following you?" I ask her, although her eyes are still on the subway tunnel and her body's still as she holds her breath.

"I don't know." Her bright blue eyes flicker to mine as she says, "I'm scared, Evan."

"You should go to the cops, Sam-" I start to tell her she needs to protect herself, and if she doesn't trust the cops she can always hire security, but she cuts me off.

"It's not me. I'm not worried about me. If he thinks you know, you're not safe."

"I don't care what he thinks. Or what he thinks I know." I stare into her eyes as I tell her, "I'll kill him before he touches me again."

CHAPTER 10

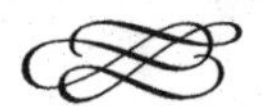

Kat

Distractions are not always wise,
And can come at the worst of times.
When you're weak and when you're lonely,
When you're suffering for your crimes.
They sound so tempting as they soothe,
All the pain of yesterday.
They'll hold you tight with promises just right,
While the truth fades from black to gray.

He knows what he's doing.

Jacob Scott.

Coffee? I could use some advice. I check out the message as I sit at a booth at the back of the coffee shop we met at last time. The new place and not my old go-to I've had for years.

My blood rings with guilt and regret. Even as I sit here, looking from the cup of chamomile tea to the door of the shop as the bell at the top of the door rings, granting entry to the tempter himself.

I should tell Jacob I'm pregnant. That I'm not at all ready to think about moving on, although I wish I were after the weeks of hell and on-again, off-again hardships Evan and I have been through. I should tell Jacob no. I should tell him sorry for not telling him sooner.

But I don't do any of that.

I give a small wave to him and then force my smile to stay put as he walks over to me. His shoulders shudder and I can feel the faint chill of the November air flow through the shop.

"I'm so glad you could come," Jacob says, shoving his jacket off of his shoulders. I smile as I see the waitress approach, carrying the cup of chai I bought for him.

"You have good timing," I tell him, biting the inside of my cheek and knowing that I'm playing with fire. "Now I don't owe you."

A genuine chuckle fills the space between us as he's given

his drink.

"Touché, Kat," he says accepting it and then thanking the barista.

I mouth the word *thanks* to her as she turns. She's sweet and young, but I don't miss how her gaze shifts to my ring finger, and then to his. She keeps her smile in place, but it doesn't reach her eyes.

My heart stutters and I wish I'd taken it off. I wish I could solidify the separation as easily as Evan walked out on me.

"You okay?" Jake asks and grabs my attention again.

"Yeah," I say and force a smile to my lips. It feels tight and I can't breathe, so I pick up the tea to take a sip.

I clear my throat and try to shake off the unwanted feelings. "Do you want a muffin?" I ask him absently. "Or a cookie?"

I read last night about all the foods you should and shouldn't eat when you're pregnant. Oatmeal seems to be a winner, so the thought of having an oatmeal raisin cookie or two is a good distraction.

"A COOKIE?" Jake smirks and I almost tell him why. But I

don't. I gesture to the front of the place; I can't be the only one who smells all the baked goods.

"You got the drinks, let me get the snacks."

"Oatmeal raisin?" I ask him and he nods with another smirk before tapping on the table and walking to the counter.

I stare down at my not-so-big-yet belly and feel slightly guilty. Pursing my lips, I think, *don't look at me like that* jokingly and it actually eases some of the pain.

At least I'm not crying and wallowing in despair. I gently rub my belly.

"At least I have you," I whisper in a sweet, sorrowful voice as I let my hand rest on my lower belly. I want a doctor to tell me it's real. That I really do get to have a baby. This little one who will love me and I can love them back and give them every part of me.

As I take another sip of the tea, watching Jake at the counter, I start to think. Maybe it was supposed to be this way. Maybe I don't have enough in me to love both a child and my husband. God must've known it and that's why Evan left me.

I nod my head and sniffle before pulling the mug back to my lips quickly to hide my face from Jake.

He sits down slowly and I know he saw; I can see it in his eyes.

"Sorry," I shrug. "I read this manuscript earlier and it shredded me," I lie.

He hands me my cookie and I feel foolish for a moment, but then he says, "Really?"

I nod like a fool.

"You want to talk about it?" he asks me and I get the impression that I could tell him anything. I think I could tell him the truth right now and he'd know it's exactly that. I could spill my guts to him and say it's all something I read in a book. And he'd let me. He'd give me that bit of protection.

And I'm so grateful for it.

But I'm not ready.

I shake my head, my hair spilling over my shoulders as I do. "Maybe another time."

He nods his head, peeling back the muffin wrapper only enough so he can take a bite.

"Good thinking," he says after he swallows. "Very good call on the muffin."

My shoulders rock gently with another small laugh as I

take a bite of the cookie, once again feeling the ease that Jake gives me.

"It's okay to not be okay, do you know that?" he asks me.

I snicker and pick at the cookie.

"You can roll your eyes and laugh, but it's true," he says as he peels down the muffin wrapper, exposing more of the treat as he talks.

"If I'm not okay though, that means I need to talk about it." I point my finger at him and then pick off another small piece of the cookie. "And I don't want to," I say smartly and pop the bit into my mouth.

"Nah, you can just be not okay, but talk about something else. That's a thing, you know?"

"How's that?" I ask him.

"It's okay to let something bother you, that's all I mean."

"You authors can speak in code, do *you* know that?" I use his phrase right back at him.

Now he's the one who laughs. "Well I guess what I'm saying is that I'm not really okay. I'm sort of running from my own problems. But now I'm okay, 'cause I'm here."

"Here in New York?"

"Just here," he says and gives me a small smile, but I read the real answer in his expression. *Here with you.*

"So what are you running from?" I ask him.

"Are we sharing stories?" he asks me in return.

"I'm not sure how much sharing I'm willing to do," I tell him honestly.

"You afraid you'll wind up in a book of mine?" he asks me with a sly smile and then adds, "One second, before you start I just wanted to grab my pen and paper."

He acts like he's reaching for an imaginary bag on the floor and I let out a loud laugh then cover my mouth with both of my hands as a lady looks up from her phone at me with a pissed off expression from across the room.

Jake liked the laugh though. Enough so that he smiles wide as he settles back into his seat.

"You don't have to tell me anything. I just want you to know that you can be not okay around me. I get it. Some days I'm not the best and it's nice to just go out and get a chai … and a muffin."

"Like today?" I ask him.

"Yeah, like today."

"I have a hard time getting a read on you, Jake," I tell him.

"What do you want to know?" he asks me.

"What do you want from me?" I ask him instantly and then immediately regret the blunt question. It's rude and risks losing him and the only distraction I really have.

"Just company, until you want more," he says with his green eyes staring straight into mine as they heat.

"I don't know that I'll want more though."

"I think you lie, Kat. I think you already know you want more."

"It's only because I'm lonely." The words slip out and I hate that they're true, but a weight is lifted from the confession. I expect Jake to react negatively. Maybe to be angry or offended, but instead he nods his head.

"Yeah I know, I am too."

"Sometimes I do stupid shit when I'm lonely."

"Well if you ever want to be lonely together, I'm free."

I should feel guilty about how Jake makes me feel.

Wanted, appreciated, like he doesn't want to lose me.

It's foolish to even entertain what's between us. But I feel so rejected. My husband doesn't want me. And yet Jake does. Even if it's only because I'm the only person in the entire state who he knows.

And we can be just friends.

At least I can pretend we can, for a little while. Or what did Evan call it? *A short while.*

UNTITLED

Diary Entry 2

Hey Mom,

I have a secret to tell you. Do you remember how I told you about Markie in middle school? He's the one who was in Mrs. Schaffer's math class. He had a crush on me and sent me that note. It wasn't important really and I doubt you remember. But I had this feeling back then and I kind of have it now.

It's weird and it's mixed with all sorts of other things.

Obviously I shouldn't see him and I shouldn't even be considering talking to this guy. But I've been crying every night for so long. I started playing sad movies on the television at night so I could blame it on that. I know I'm lying, but I'm so tired of crying.

I'm exhausted, Mom, and this guy gives me something else to think about.

It's wrong, isn't it?

I don't even have to ask you to know that it is.

I'm using this guy, and I'm still married to Evan. My heart is still waiting for him even though he's given me every reason to stay away from him for good.

Maybe I'm a bad person. Maybe I deserve all this.

I don't know. Could you tell me, please? You used to give me little signs. I know they were from you. I could use one now.

I don't know what's going to happen. But I'm really tired and that's probably from a mix of what's going on with Evan and the pregnancy.

It's wonderful that we're having a baby, isn't it?

See how I changed subjects there? I hope that made you laugh.

I'm happy about this baby and I want to feel happy, Mom.

But my life isn't happy and I kind of hate myself right now.

This guy changes that. Does that make it better?

Please tell me it does, because I want it all to be better for the baby.

I know it can't last, but maybe just for a little while?

CHAPTER 11

Evan

Dominos fall one by one,
Yet together look the same.
The white and black blur to gray,
It's only a child's game.
They tip and spill on the ground,
Claiming that they've won.
Lined up in rows, touching toes,
Dominos fall one by one.

"It's been a while," Mason says as I sit down at the booth in the back of the restaurant.

"I just saw you a few weeks ago," I point out to him.

"Not what I meant," he corrects me. "It's been a while since the two of us have been up to no good."

"And how do you know that's what I'm here for?" I ask him. I used to buy some good shit through Mason and vice versa. I came from the poor part of town, and him from the rich. The only real difference that makes is which drugs you're doing. Pot or snow.

And if you want a taste of the other, all you have to do is make friends with the right people. Long story short, that's how I met Mason and as I moved into his circle, he made a spot when I needed one.

Mason shrugs at my question. "I'm going to take a guess and say that whatever you want from me, it's something I could go to jail for."

I huff a sarcastic laugh and toss my phone down on the white tablecloth then look around casually to make sure I don't recognize anyone. The place is mostly empty, with only a few guys at the bar and a couple in the corner of the diner.

"We're good," Mason says. "And I have to say, considering what's going on, I'm intrigued."

"Intrigued is a word for it, I guess," I answer him.

"I got you an IPA, seasonal."

"Thanks, man," I tell him gratefully but I don't touch the tall glass sitting right in front of me. I take off my coat and hang it over the unused chair to my left as the waitress walks up to the table. She's a skinny little thing, which makes her look even younger than she probably is.

"Welcome to Murray's," she says evenly as she pours water into each of our glasses. Her top's unbuttoned just a little too much and the way the blush colors her cheeks as she looks between us makes what she's thinking more than obvious.

"Can I get you guys anything?" she asks, setting the pitcher down. She bites down on her lip and Mason raises a brow at me.

"Not me," I tell him and lean back in my seat, not looking back at the broad and risking leading her on.

He waves her off politely. "We'll just grab a drink from the bar," he tells her and her smile falls. She seems to falter and she clears her throat.

"Sure, if you need anything—" she starts to say, but he cuts her off.

"We're good."

"So how you been?" I ask him as the pretty little blonde walks off with a pout.

"Better now," he tells me.

"I'm sorry to hear about your father."

He shrugs and looks away as he takes a long swig of his beer.

"I know it's got to suck either way," I say my words carefully. Word is Mason killed him. Shot him dead. But still, it's his father and I don't know for a fact Mason really wanted him gone.

"Yeah," he says, not looking me in the eyes. "Thanks, but let's cut the small talk. It's not often I get a call from you."

I nod and crack my knuckles one by one with my thumb as I look out the window, scanning the streets. "I think I need to hire someone," I tell him.

"You're going to need to be a little more specific than that," he replies.

"There's someone," I pause and lean in closer, resting my elbow on the table and moving my hand so that my fingers cover my mouth as I talk. Just in case someone's watching and trying to listen in.

"Someone tried to kill me. Tony wasn't meant to die. It was meant for me."

"You're still doing coke?" he asks and eyes me then takes a drink from his glass.

"Not in years, but they don't know that. It would hurt my reputation if the clients thought I was clean, you know?"

"That's what I thought. I was just asking 'cause that means whoever went for you doesn't really know you."

"I think it's my boss."

"Wouldn't he know?" he asks me and for a moment a tinge of insecurity washes through me.

"He never really asked. He doesn't ask any questions so long as the clients are happy."

"Alright." He tilts his head slightly and lowers his voice. "So why's he want you dead?" Mason asks.

"It was years ago," I start to tell him and feel sick to my stomach. "I fucked his wife. Before I married Kat."

Mason's eyes assess me as if he's trying to figure out if I'm lying.

"I've never cheated on her," I talk louder than I should and in response to my raised voice, Mason looks to his right.

I lick my lips and calm my racing heart.

"He wants to scare her, so he went after me to prove what he could do to her. That no one's safe from him."

"But you gave Tony the hit?"

I nod my head once, the memory of his dead eyes looking through me flashing in front of me and sending a chill down my spine. "With the stuff James left in the room for me."

"So your boss? You want him dead? You want to prove he did it, frame him, what do you want?"

"You have a fucking menu?" I joke with him to lessen the tension in my body.

An asymmetrical grin forms on his face.

"I don't do anything. I'm not involved in any of that shit anymore."

My body feels heavier at his words.

"Doesn't mean I don't have connections still," he adds and I nod. "So, for a friend, what is it that you want?"

"Three things," I tell him. "First, your lawyer."

"That's a given. He's already on call in case they take you in again."

"Second, someone to watch Kat. I need her safe."

"Is he after her?" he asks me.

"He might know that I know, and I can't risk her safety." He merely nods and I add, "I can't lose her. I'll fucking lose it, man."

"The safest place for her is distance. Well, anywhere fucking away from you and your shit."

"I know … I know."

"Good thing you're separated, huh?"

"She tell Jules that?" I ask him as dread races in my blood. Before I can tell him we're not, and that there's no way I'm leaving her, he laughs at me.

"Jules tells me everything. I know the papers got it wrong."

"I'm not leaving her; I'm just protecting her. There's a difference."

"If you want the world to think you're broken up," he says, "then you need to treat her like you are."

"I don't know if I can treat her like that. She's pregnant."

"I know she is. Doesn't that make it even more important not to risk?" he asks me.

"Don't make me feel worse than I already do." My words are bitter and my heart sinks. "How long's it going to take?" I ask him to get back to the point.

"To dig up dirt, plant evidence, figure out how to kill the guy … it could be a while."

"I don't have a while," I bite back. "Every day is a day I

have to put her through this. What if she hates me?" I say out loud even though I didn't mean to.

"There are worse things you could do," Mason says and my attention returns to him.

"I can't lose her," I tell him and he nods his head.

"I'll watch her myself," he offers and a small sense of peace relaxes me, but only a fraction of the way.

I rub my eyes with the back of my hand and finally pick up the beer on the table.

"If anything happens to her ... "

"Nothing's going to happen to her," he reassures me before asking, "And what's the third thing?"

I look him in the eyes and tell him, "I want him to go to jail for what he did. Whether you get real evidence or have to create some. And if that's not possible, I want James Lapour dead."

CHAPTER 12

Kat

Lonely isn't so bad,
There's life within, you see.
There's faith and so much more to come,
With the fate of what's to be.
The memories that haunt the night,
Die in time as the sky turns cold.
There's hope that comes in morning,
And a day that's left to be told.

"I THOUGHT you were taking time off?" Sue says and brings me back to the present.

I didn't even hear her come in. I glance at the clock in the upper right of my computer screen. It's already five o'clock and time for our dinner date. The girls are taking turns keeping me occupied. It's almost like they're babysitting me and if it was anyone else, I'd hate it.

But I can never turn down a date with Suzette.

"You of all people should know that working is all I'm good for." My voice comes out flat although I meant for it to be funny. God, I'm tired. I'm always tired now even though I'm finally starting to sleep like the dead.

I guess the first trimester of pregnancy will do that to you.

"Oh honey, have you not looked at your shoe collection recently?" she asks, quirking a brow. "You're good for so much more than work."

I stand up slowly, letting my body stretch as I do and smile at her. "Ha-ha," I say sarcastically, but the smile on my lips is genuine.

"So, what place tonight?" she asks as she turns on a lamp in the corner of the office and settles into the one comfy chair in the room … which isn't even the desk chair.

"Order in, takeout, getting pretty and hitting the town?" she suggests then takes her scarf off slowly and looks around the office.

"Why the hell haven't you decorated this room?" she asks me before I can answer the first question. I scratch the back of my head as I look around. I have a bookshelf in the back, but all the books are still in boxes on the floor.

"Just not a priority," I tell her honestly. "I look at the screen more than anything anyway."

"It's like your décor inspiration was a depressing cubicle."

I snort at her response, but it makes me laugh so hard.

"Maddie should focus on redecorating in here before planning a baby shower."

I think the remark wasn't meant to be taken seriously, but I actually love the idea.

"I should tell her. I'd like that."

Sue shrugs, twisting the scarf around her hand as she crosses her legs. "I'm sure she'd love to."

"Well, actually. I totally forgot to tell you, but I may move in with Jules for a little while."

Sue leans forward with her mouth a bit more open than it should be before she says, "You sure you want to have to hear them when they fuck? I feel like that's the number one concern here."

I roll my eyes at her. "It was Mason's suggestion, so I'm

sure he ... " *Ugh.* The thought of them doing it in the room next to me is a thought I'd rather not picture.

"I get it," Sue says, sensing exactly what was on my mind. "You shouldn't be alone anyway. Not when you have so many people who love you."

I shut down my laptop and just give her a tight smile.

She adds, "'Cause you're not alone, and there's no reason you should feel it right now."

"Damn it Sue, stop it," I tell her and shake off the emotions as they creep up on me. "I'm fine."

"I know you are!" she says, pushing herself up from the seat. "And that's why we're going to go out and go somewhere fabulous."

My phone dings on the desk, indicating a text as I start to tell Sue that I don't really want to go out.

I let out a yawn as I cautiously look at the message. I've had four texts today already. Each from a gossip column editor wanting a statement on my reaction to the recent events. Evan's been spotted with Samantha again and the rumor mill is churning with tales of scandal.

They can go fuck themselves. I believe that was my response for each of the columnists. Probably not the best quote I've ever given.

"You okay?" Sue asks and I nod when I see it's just from Henry.

He keeps messaging me, which makes the fact that Evan hasn't bothered to call me back that much harder to take.

"Just Evan's dad. Wanting to drop by with some lemons."

"Lemons?" she questions.

"He said they helped Marie when she was pregnant and nauseated."

"But you aren't . . . " Sue trails off with a hint of confusion.

"I know!" I answer jokingly as I text Henry, *Thank you, but I'm fine.* I question if I should ask him how Evan is. Where he is. Or anything at all.

Before I can, he answers that he wants to meet up for lunch soon.

"You know, he's real sweet," I tell Sue, feeling guilty and torn on what to do.

"So where'd his son get his charm from then?" Sue asks sarcastically and then mouths that she's sorry when she sees I'm not amused.

"I'll just tell him I will, but I can always bail," I say out loud as if I need her approval.

"Yeah, that's a good way to handle it," she says and then

looks me up and down. "You should probably put real clothes on."

"How fancy?" I ask her, setting the phone down as I realize I'm still in sweats and a baggy t-shirt.

"Let's go fancy fancy." I hope she can see how the thought of getting prettied up makes me perk up. I could really use a night out, feeling beautiful and carefree. A nice distraction.

"Fancy-pantsing it up tonight?" I ask her, already feeling better than I did before she got here.

"You know it."

CHAPTER 13

Evan

Hold back the anger,
For it makes you blind.
Hold back your revenge,
It clouds and fogs your mind.
The secrets left in shadows,
Drift closer in the night.
They leave you left with nothing,
Only monsters left to fight.

All I can focus on are his tells.

You learn them fast in the line of business that led me to

this moment. The sweat on his brow. The way his foot won't stay still. His dilated pupils and quick breathing.

He's one of two things. High as a fucking kite, or going through withdrawal.

And judging by the look on this fucker's face, James Lapour is ready for his next hit.

I peek over my shoulder. His office is on the first floor. There are apartments above us and plenty of witnesses in case some shit goes down. But just outside those doors is Mason, sitting in a car and waiting for me in case I need him.

I've got two goals coming in here like this.

1. Warn him to back the fuck off.
2. Get any evidence I can.

Seeing as how he's in his office, goal number two will have to wait unless I can get a confession. I slip the tape recorder on, and do everything I can to keep my hate down. But the image of Kat from the night terrors is all I can see. I can't sleep; I can't do anything without thinking about losing her. I feel like I'm losing my sanity. I have to hesitate and focus. Blinking away the picture of her, I prepare to do what I have to.

"Taking a break from the snow?" I ask him as I walk into

the room. I've been standing outside the open door to his office just watching him for a few minutes. He didn't change the locks and there's no one else here on a late Wednesday night. Just him and me. Well not quite, there are a few broads in the far back. I can hear them from here. Maybe they're waiting for him with exactly what he needs. I wouldn't be surprised.

"What the fuck are you doing here?" he sneers at me.

"I just want to know why, really." I say the words easily as I walk closer to him. The city lights outside give the room a glow, but with the blinds drawn and only the lamp on his desk illuminating the space, it's darker than I'd like it to be in here.

"Why what exactly?" he asks me, leaning back in his seat and I can faintly hear him pulling out a drawer slowly.

I rack the slide on the gun in my hand and raise it slowly. "Uh, uh, uh," I reprimand him. It's been a long fucking time since I've aimed a gun at someone. I've never wanted to pull the trigger more though.

"I wouldn't do anything fast if I were you," I tell him.

He raises his hands slowly, cocking his head and letting out a sick laugh. "So you here to kill me now? Is that it?"

"I should, shouldn't I?"

"For what, exactly? Spit it out, you coward," he scoffs at me. His eyes are so bloodshot, they're nearly black with the lack of light.

"I'm the coward?" I ask him with ridicule. I have to be careful with the loaded gun. I nearly point it at myself like a dumbass. My anger is putting me on edge, my adrenaline pumping hard and every second that passes makes my body temperature go up just a little more.

One of the girls from the back room yells out, "You alright in there?" in response to my raised voice.

Before I can say shit, James answers them. "Just stay where you're put." Good old James, he knows how to talk to the ladies.

"What do you want, Evan?" he asks me, slowly laying his hands on the desk, palms down.

His arm twitches and I can tell he's fucked up.

"What's going on with you?" I ask him. "You're not looking so good."

"You look pretty fucked yourself," he tells me, forcing a smile onto his face.

"We saw you watching," I tell him.

"What's that?" he asks.

"At Rockefeller Center."

"Is that so?" I hate this game he's playing. This tit for tat where no real information is given. "And what exactly was I watching?" he asks with a smirk on his face although I can see in his eyes that he's curious.

I shrug and say, "Doesn't matter, does it? What I want to know is what you plan on doing."

He laughs abruptly, deep and from his gut, but any trace of happiness is immediately replaced with pain. He nearly doubles over and I raise the gun again, my heart beating hard as I prepare for him to come up with a weapon.

He doesn't though and when he sees the gun aimed right between his eyes, he forces his hands in the air again.

"You stop doing coke? I guess Tony told you it was bad for you," I tell him flatly, swallowing thickly as my hands sweat and the gun feels heavier.

He groans an answer I can't hear and then he winces again.

"What the fuck is wrong with you? Withdrawal?"

"Fuck you," he manages to get out.

"You paranoid now? That someone's going to do to you what you tried to do to me?"

He opens his eyes slowly, the light shining from the lamp creating shadows on his face. "The fuck you talking about?"

"The coke you laced. You scared someone's going to do the same to you? Give you what you have coming?"

"It was my personal stash, you prick."

I almost call him a liar, I almost tell him to shove it and put a bullet in his chest so I can get back to Kat and end this shit. But the look on his face stops me.

He's always been a damn good liar though.

"If I wanted you dead … well, I know how to use a gun."

"You want to know what I think?" I ask him, although I already know the answer.

"Sure, you can say that I'm intrigued," he retorts.

"I think you're greedy," I tell him as I lower the gun.

"Greedy?" he says back with a crooked smile.

"I think you wanted to prove a point to your wife." I lay it out there for him. I'm not messing around; I want this prick to know that I'm fully aware of what he's doing.

"That bitch, she's got nothing to do with this."

"Who does then?" I ask him.

His bottom lip lowers, but then his mouth slams shut. "Fuck you."

"I won't stop until I find out everything. Until every bit of dirt I can get on you is dug up and exposed."

"You know how much shit I've got on you, Thompson?" He seems to find his strength as he leans forward on his desk.

"This is a warning to stay away. From me and Samantha." I almost bring up Kat. I almost say she's pregnant. That family's off-limits. But that would only give him that much more of a reason to hurt her. So I keep her name out of my mouth, I keep her safe.

"So it's true then?" he asks with a snort of a laugh. "You two are together?"

With the visions of Kat in my head, I almost think he's talking about her. That he knows we're back together. It takes me a moment before I realize he's talking about Samantha and referring to the rumors. Thank fuck. "She came to me for help."

"I always knew she'd cross me. I didn't think you'd be the dumb fuck she picked to go down with her."

I raise the gun and take a step closer. "Give me one reason I shouldn't kill you right now. You and I both know you deserve it."

He shrugs. "I have the evidence that proves you lied to the cops, for one. I have evidence on both you assholes."

"A dead man can't do shit with evidence."

"The cops will find it, and you know it. You don't want them messing around in here."

"What are you doing back here, baby?" A high-pitched voice rings through the hallway and I look quickly over my shoulder. I hear the door open and James smiles.

"Oh yeah, there are two other reasons. In all the years I've known you, you've never put your hands on a woman. Well other than Sam, I mean."

"Shut the fuck up," I spit out through my clenched teeth.

"Come on back, baby!" he yells out. He's calling my bluff and I'm quick to put the gun down, hiding it behind my leg.

My heart beats slowly and I can see it all playing out. Killing this fucker and the two of them screaming, running. I can see the red, blue, and white lights, reflecting off the glass.

"Are you ready for us?" A young woman walks in, skinny as a rail with a sharp blonde bob. It looks so perfectly straight, I think it's a wig.

The smell of perfume floods the room as she walks in, swaying her hips and wearing shorts that ride up her ass.

Hookers.

"Let me just finish this conversation real quick," James says and the second girl walks in a bit behind the first. The blonde rounds the desk, peeking at me, but stalks toward James to perch on the corner of his desk.

"Whatever you want. I'm not in a rush."

"Hi there," a little brunette says. Her voice is softer, sweeter even, which matches her look. She's got a vibe that's more innocent, with clothes that actually cover her ass. But her eyes are bloodshot and she can barely walk straight. She tries to lean against me, but I take a step back and when I do she sees my gun.

Her eyes widen and she stumbles backward with a gasp. The two girls exchange a look while holding their breath, both of them on edge and realizing they shouldn't have walked back here.

"I was just on my way out," I tell them slowly. I don't need them calling the cops and getting my ass locked up for some dumb shit. I tuck the gun back into the waist of my jeans.

"I just want to ask one question before you leave, Thompson," James says to my back as I turn away.

"So wives aren't off-limits anymore, are they?" he asks. My blood rushes into my ears and I almost do it. I almost kill that fucker, consequences be damned.

"Ah, I see not all the rumors are true. Are they, Evan?"

"Leave her the fuck alone, James." My blood pumps hot as I stare into his beady eyes. But all he does is smile.

And that's what I dream about tonight. The piece of the nightmare that I've added. His fucking smile while I hold my wife's dead body.

CHAPTER 14

Kat

Just hold on a bit longer,
I'm not ready for you to go.
I made mistakes, I didn't say—
Come back, for you should know.
I didn't tell you I loved you,
Or that I'm sorry I didn't stay.
I wasn't true to you or me,
And now you've gone away.

It's been three days now.

And Evan hasn't texted or come back.

I texted and called, remembering how he said he loved me and this was only going to last for a short while. It was pathetic of me.

I'm lonely, emotional, pregnant. I was desperate to believe he still loved me.

The text was simple. *It's really hard without you. I'm sorry; I was wrong to give you an ultimatum. Please forgive me. I miss you and I really need you.* That's what being lonely does to me. It makes me wish he'd just come back to me.

And I got nothing back.

I thought it would get easier, but somehow Evan refusing to text me back is making it harder. He doesn't return my calls. Nothing. The only contact I have with him is an excerpt from the Page Six column quoting him as saying that we've split.

I keep remembering how he said it was just for a "short while." Maybe that's how he got me. He left me with hope.

That fucking bastard.

It's like my body doesn't want to hate him and instead the blame is falling on me.

It's my fault I pushed him away.

My fault I gave him an ultimatum.

Why am I the one hoping he'll forgive me?

Why am I the one praying he'll write me back, leaving voicemails saying he's sorry?

At least at night. And only late at night.

The days are so much easier.

After the unanswered texts, I started packing his shit into boxes.

And then I moved out and into Jules' guest room.

I moved out … of an empty house. What the fuck is wrong with me?

I don't know if I'm insane, hormonal, or how the hell I'm supposed to react to all this.

The only thing I really know is that I'm not the first woman to have a man leave her. I won't be the last, either.

It is what it is, and every second that goes by with Evan not saying a word is one more scale on my armor hardening.

"What about her?" Jules asks me and I lift my gaze to her, trying not to show how pissed off I am. It's not her fault.

She's cuddled up on the couch, a cream and soft brown striped throw over her legs with the computer in her lap. She faces it toward me and I check out the profile.

Personal Assistant – Angela Kent

She has experience and an impressive resume. My eyes scan down the lines on the screen, but it's hard for me to focus. I know I need to do some interviews and hire someone to help me. Or take on less work from the agency. Both are viable options. I just need to pick one. And hopefully soon. I'm drowning in work, but struggling to do anything.

"Maybe," I tell her and then lean back into the sofa. I let my head fall back and wish I had one thing figured out in my life. Just one.

It seems like nothing can go right anymore.

"Hey, come on," Jules says and places the laptop on the ottoman so she can scoot forward and lean against the armrest of my chair. "It's going to be okay. No matter how dark the night gets, the sun will come in the morning." She gives me this soft, encouraging smile for me to cheer up. It's one of the lines from her first book she gave me as her agent. The memory takes me back to the high point of my life and then it crushes me.

"I'm sorry," I tell her. "It's just that the nights are hard."

"I get that," she says. "Do you want me to make you some tea?"

I shake my head no. "I think I just need to sleep," I tell her, but I really don't know what I need and that's the problem. There's no solution to this problem because it's out of my control.

"If he said he's coming back, I guess the real question is, do you wait for him?"

"I told him it's over." I sniff and absently pick at a fray on the end of the throw. "I told him if he walked out, I was done."

"I know what you said. But it's obviously not over, not for you."

I mutter lowly, "I would be stupid to take him back."

Jules smirks at me as she says, "We've all done stupid things. Haven't we?"

She talks as she stands, letting the throw fall to the floor so she can stretch her back and adds, "Besides, forgiveness isn't stupid and neither is love." She says the words so confidently and lightheartedly, as if they're so obviously true.

"Can I beat the shit out of him first?" I peek up at her with a half-grin, feeling a bit upbeat just from her being with me.

"I think I'll allow it," she responds as her own smile grows.

Mason's footsteps can be heard from down the hall. He's not quiet in the least and part of me wonders if he wants us to know he's coming. "Sweetheart?" he calls out and we both turn to the open doorway before he enters.

"You wanna come to bed?" he asks Jules, gripping both sides of the doorway molding then leans in, just his upper half in the room. Like he's checking to see if he's welcome.

"I don't know," Jules says, but then immediately yawns.

"Go to bed, I'll be fine," I tell her and wave her off. "I'm tired too."

"It might be silly," Jules says as Mason walks toward her and wraps his arm around her waist, "but I'm really happy you're here."

"Thanks," I reply and mean it. Such a simple admission makes my heart swell. That's how badly I need someone right now.

"I'm lucky I have you," I tell her. "And I guess you too," I tell Mason, suddenly feeling awkward that he's in the mix of this chick lovefest.

"You staying up?" he asks me.

"I'm exhausted. I think I'm just going to watch something and pass out."

"I can stay up with you," Jules offers, and her voice is even peppy. She's eager to help me. But she's not the one I need.

"I'm good. Seriously," I tell her easily and for a moment I think I will be when she yields and they say goodnight. But as their footsteps slowly quiet to nothing, and the television proves useless for a good distraction, I start to remember what happened only nights ago.

How I opened my heart to Evan, while it was raw and damaged from his own doing.

And how accepted I felt when he said he was happy we were having a baby. Not just accepted, but complete and whole and like everything was going to be better than okay.

How loved I felt when he held me and kissed me.

How I didn't want to be anything other than *his* when he laid me down in bed.

I think that's the part that hurts the most. I would give up everything to just be his.

And he can't even text me back. Not even today when I was scared shitless thinking someone was following me on my way to the company office for a short meeting. It was hard enough trying to keep my composure for the full two hours. I didn't say anything the entire time. But on the way back home, I felt a pair of eyes on me. It was like a prickle at the base of my neck, like a sixth sense that told me someone was following me.

I hailed a cab and texted Evan immediately. Out of habit more than anything else.

I feel like I'm going crazy, with paranoia and all the hormones and crazy emotions coming with pregnancy. But I'm at least honest with Evan and open and raw. If nothing else I'm giving him everything I have to offer. And he can't even give me a text.

I pick up my phone, intent on texting him just that.

He can ignore me all he wants, but I'm going to tell him everything I feel. I deserve that much. To at least be able to tell him. *I'm not the one who keeps secrets. I'm not perfect,* I text him. *I'm slowing down at work. I have to. Carrying your baby is making me so tired. I love being pregnant though. I love knowing we're going to have a baby.* But I'm afraid I'm hurting him by being this way. I don't know how to get better though.

I delete the last bit and stare at the ceiling as tears threaten to come.

I used to do this when my parents died. I used to write to them like I did at camp. I'd write to them telling them how angry I was. How they needed to come back.

It's not fair that Evan is alive and says he wants me. Yet a very large piece of my heart feels like I've lost him forever.

Please, Evan. Please come back to me.

Just as I delete all the words, my phone rings.

It's a number I don't recognize and I let it ring again in my hand before answering it.

"Hello?"

"Hello. This is Dr. Pierce. I'm so sorry to call you, but Mr. Thompson's phone has you listed as his daughter. Is that right?"

At first I'm confused, thinking Evan's in the hospital, but then I realize it's his father, Henry, that the doctor is referring to.

"Are you calling from a hospital?" I ask him as I sit up straighter, my mind waking up from the fog it was just in. Rather than correcting the doctor and telling him that I'm Henry's daughter-in-law and soon-to-be ex-daughter-in-law at that, I question him by asking, "Is everything alright?"

The doctor exhales on the other end of the line, but it's not out of exhaustion or boredom, it's the type of exhalation that accompanies bad news. The kind of sigh that says, *I'm so sorry, I wish I didn't have to tell you.*

"I would like to first apologize for having to speak to you over the phone," the doctor says and I'm taken back to middle school. Sitting down in the principal's office, wondering what I did. I sat there, my legs swinging nervously as he brought in the secretary and then gave me such a sad look before leaving the room. He was so sorry to tell me. They're always so sorry to tell you.

No one wants to be in the room when you learn your parents have died. No one wants to be the person to tell you. I could see it in Mrs. Carsen's eyes.

"Sorry to tell me what?" I ask the doctor, but I'm already prepared for it. My heart feels both swollen and hollow and my head light with denial. I lower myself to the floor, my hand shaking as I hold the phone to my ear.

"Mr. Thompson suffered a blood clot, and unfortunately, it traveled to his lungs."

I remember the way the bell rang as I cried and the other students ran through the halls, moving on with their lives and not knowing my life had changed forever in that moment.

The same agonizing pain rips through me and the tears fall freely as I end the call.

He can't be dead. Not Henry.

He was the only dad I had, and I threw him away. He was supposed to be with me tonight. Like he wanted.

If I had met him, if I hadn't blown him off … Regret consumes me.

I can hardly breathe as the phone drops next to me and I cover my face. He didn't deserve to die. It's an odd thing to think, because it means others do. But Evan's father should still be here. He wasn't supposed to go. Not yet.

My body shudders as I hold back a sob.

I've cried so many tears over the past weeks. So many shed on my pillow, in my hands, soaking into my heated skin.

But these tears are different.

It's not from a fear of loss. It's not because I'm disappointed in myself. It's not even because I'm hopeless.

When you shed tears over something that's truly gone, those are the tears that never leave you. It drowns your soul and takes a piece of your heart. That's what death does.

I have to force myself to text Evan. *Call me as soon as you can.*

I don't want to tell him over the phone. I want to be there for him. To hold him and ease the pain. Even more, I need him to hold me.

I hesitate but then add, *It's about your father.*

The phone shifts out of focus as my eyes blur and my hand shakes, but I hear it ping after only a small moment.

It's not Evan though, it's Jake.

Hey, you want a coffee? he asks and I have to force myself not to message him. I have to force myself not to tell him that I'm not okay. That I can admit it and that it hurts.

But after almost an hour going by and a dozen more text messages unanswered from Evan, I cave. I have to tell him, and so I do. I tell him over a text that his father passed away and after crying for hours and seeing that he read it, I still get nothing back.

I text Jake, *I'm not okay.*

CHAPTER 15

Evan

She won't wait for you forever,
There's no way she ever could.
Time changes by the day and life,
Brings both the bad and good.
It creeps into who you are,
And deep down in your soul.
The person that you left behind,
Will never again be whole.

IT'S FITTING that it would snow today. My shoulders shudder as I watch the men dig the hole that my father will be laid in tomorrow. The ground's hard and stubborn. Like my father, in a way.

The frigid air isn't doing shit to help me keep my composure. I have to sniff and shove my hands in my pockets as I kick the ground.

All day, all I could think is that it was James who somehow found a way to kill my pops. Mason's the only reason I didn't go back into his office and kill him. Even if he wasn't there, there's not a place he could run.

I'm paranoid. I'm desperate. I'm fucking lonely.

I want my wife. I need her. And a weak man would go to her. *And make her a target.*

The snow crunches on my right and I turn toward the small parking lot. Mason's early. I didn't even hear him come up behind me.

"Thanks for coming, man," I tell him and take his outstretched hand.

"I'm so sorry," Mason tells me as takes a look behind me at the gravesite. He found Kat downstairs and he's the one who told me.

Every piece of me is begging to go to her. She can make me feel better–not right, but better.

"Anything suspicious?" I ask Mason as I turn from the

two men digging the hole. I'm desperate for someone to blame this on. It's hard to even think it's real, let alone just an accident. I'll fucking lose it if he says yes, but that's what I'm praying for. I'm already on edge. The anger is so much easier to handle than the despair. If this was because of me, I'll never forgive myself. My heart clenches as Mason stares back at me.

"It was natural causes," he says with more sorrow than I anticipated. I have to turn from him and face the nearly empty parking lot as the wind whips in my face.

I bite back the need to cry and simply nod my head.

Just a blood clot. Just bad luck. There's no one to blame or kill.

And that's what hurts the most.

"I'm really sorry," Mason says behind me. He gives me the space I need and I'm grateful for it.

"Your girl," Mason starts and then clears his throat. "You've got to do something for her." His voice is weak, like he's begging me.

"You're the one who said I can't," I tell him as I face him. He told me not to. To not even think about texting her back. James is tracking my phone, just like we're tracking his.

"When I asked about her being followed, and you said it wasn't your guy," I remind him.

"This is different," Mason tells me like it wasn't a big deal that someone could've been watching her.

"She's not doing too well," he tells me and my eyes dart to his. My blood turns to ice as I wait for him to spit it out. *Not her*. I swallow thickly.

"She said 'everyone in her life dies,' she said that this morning," Mason tells me with a deep crease in his forehead. "She needs someone."

"You're the one who said she has to believe it too. That we're over with."

"I know, I know," Mason concedes.

"So which is it?" I practically yell.

"I'm sorry, I just … it's rough seeing her like this." I want to rip my fucking hair out. I can't stand it. This is fucking torture.

"My mistake, man, I'm sorry. Jules is there. She's not going to leave her. Just … just wait a little longer."

"How much longer?" I ask him, feeling torn and frustrated and like I can't win either way. Defeated. I feel so damn defeated.

"We don't have shit. Lapour's record is clean and there's no evidence of anything. We'll have to plant it. Including messing with his emails and credit card data."

"How long?" I ask him, not bothering to hide the irritation in my voice.

"Only days."

Days … I can wait days. It's only a few days and then everything will be right again and I'll make it better. I nod, pacing in a short circle. Just days.

"I'm afraid after what happened in his office," I tell Mason. "The way he asked about her. Like he was planning some shit."

"She's safe. I have her locked away with Jules and she doesn't even know it."

"Locked away?" I question, stopping in my tracks.

"No one's getting into that house. And Jules knows not to take her out. If Kat wants to go somewhere," Mason snaps his finger, "there's a security detail on her the second the door is opened."

"So she's safe?" I ask him. Knowing she's alright makes not being with her a little easier to swallow. She's protected, and that's all that matters. I can't lose her too.

"She's safe and not a target," Mason answers me.

"I don't know. Not after the other night. You sure she's not on his radar?"

"We're tracking his emails and calls and her name hasn't been mentioned. Yours is though."

I snort at the idea of James planning some hit on me. "And what's he saying?"

"Wants eyes on you. Wants to know what you're doing and who you're seeing."

My heart sinks at the thought. "Who I'm seeing," I echo, feeling crushed. It's like he wants me to have to stay away from her.

"Yeah," Mason answers with a defeated tone.

"That's what I needed to hear, and I won't risk it. I can't." My resolve hardens, but it sends a shooting pain down my chest. I twist the wedding ring on my finger and look back to the grave.

"Call her at least?" Mason suggests as I watch the men shoveling piles of dirt. "Not with your phone. From someone else's." I barely register Mason's words.

"If I see her or talk to her," my words come out as numb as my body feels, "I don't know how I'll walk away again."

"It's a tough call," Mason says faintly.

"She's not at risk now?" I ask him again. It's fucked up, but part of me wants her to already be in the line of fire. Just so I can go to her. To hold her, and take back everything. And I hate myself for even thinking that for a second. I'm weak. I need to be stronger for her.

DIARY ENTRY 1

DEAR POPS,

I'VE SEEN Kat do this a few times.

Writing a letter to talk to her parents. It's how I knew back then that she wasn't doing too well. I'd give her extra love and keep a closer eye on her whenever she took out that journal. I'm not doing too well now and I need you. Thought I'd give this a try; I don't have anything else.

I miss you already.

If you're with Ma, tell her I miss her too. That I love her and wish you two were here.

God, I do. I need you two.

I'm sorry I wasn't there. I'm sorry I wasn't a better son.

I'm so damn sorry that the last conversation we had was about how disappointed you were in me. I promise I'm trying to do what's right. It's so hard to know though.

It's too many lies to know what the truth is. Too many secrets to hold on to what's real.

I'm just afraid of losing everything. It's like it's all crumbling around me and I can't stop it.

I'm so damn alone, and it's my fault. I'm terrified to be close to anyone right now.

I need you to do me a favor. You gotta look out for Kat.

She misses you too and she's not okay.

She used to say that when she'd write, her parents would come in some way. She said she knew they were watching. She knew they heard. I hope you can hear me now.

Can you go to her? Please?

Give her a sign that you're there and that you love her.

I'm trying, Pops, but it's so hard to know if I'm doing the right thing.

If I lose her too, it's over for me. There's nothing left.

So please, don't watch over me. Stay with her.

I love you forever.

CHAPTER 16

Kat

It's memories that hold me back,
The visions of yesterday.
Back when we were so happy,
And our faith did not yet stray.
It's nights that I'm so lonely,
And wishing you were here.
Then the pain turns to anger,
And hating you seems so clear.

"THANKS FOR MEETING ME HERE," I say.

"No problem," Jake says as he sits down across the booth. "Tired of the chai?" he asks and I have to laugh.

We're back at Brew Madison and not the café closer to Jake's place.

"No, it's just that Jules, my friend who I'm staying with for a bit, wanted to meet across the street after we're done, so I asked her driver take me here."

"Ah, gotcha. What are you guys doing?" he asks as he looks up at the menu across the black wall. It's a large black chalkboard with all their drinks written in pretty flowing script. I'm pretty sure it's not actually handwritten. But I could be wrong.

"The chai is better at your place," I tell him and pick up my caffeine-free pumpkin spice coffee. Apparently Maddie's tastes have rubbed off on me. Either that or the baby has ruined my taste buds.

He chuckles as I take a large gulp and then tell him, "I think we're just getting dinner at a little Italian place. Or maybe heading to the new bar below the hotel a few blocks over." I shrug and add, "She hasn't decided yet."

He lays his coat over the back of his chair as he stands. "I'm going to go with straight black coffee I think."

"Oh?" I ask him. "Is it one of those days?"

"You tell me," he responds and instantly my smile falls. It's been a week since Henry died and each day is worse than "one of those days." They blur together and time has flown by, but it's really been a week.

"Give me a sec?" he asks me, gripping the back of the chair. I nod, not trusting myself to speak.

My fingers play at the edge of my coffee cup. I wore lipstick today and the outline of my lips mars the white rim of the cup.

There's a statistic I read once about how lipstick sales and alcohol sales both go up in depressions, while sales for everything else plummet.

The alcohol … well, you drink when you're happy and you drink when you're sad.

But the lipstick is because in hard times, we just want to feel special, pretty. We want to feel like we're worth it. As in, if we look pretty and put together, then maybe we can be.

I need to buy more lipstick, I think.

"So what's going on?"

"Wow, that was fast," I say to prolong my answer.

"I'd rate them an A plus for the service. I have to admit that," he answers with a pleasant smile.

I give him a soft one in return, but I can feel myself

breaking down.

"Evan's father died." As I say the words quickly, to get them out of me, my face crumples.

"Shit," I hear Jake say beneath his breath as I try to keep my composure. "It's alright," he tells me.

"I'm fine," I say in a choked voice, refusing to cry again. "I'm dealing with it. It's not the first time I've lost a family member, but it still hurts."

"What happened?"

"It was sudden. He had a blood clot that traveled to his lungs." I remember the voice of the doctor and how calmly he spoke as I pick up a napkin off the table and blot under my eyes. As I blink, my lashes hit the napkin and it comes back black.

"I'm sorry I'm such a mess," I tell him, flipping the napkin to the other side and being careful not to smudge my makeup too much.

"Don't be." It's only then that I realize how close he is. He's so warm. "Evan," I blurt out his name as my tired eyes feel heavy and the need to be held makes my body hot. My fingers itch to lay across Jake's lap. "I tried to call him and got his voicemail."

"About his father?" Jake asks and I find myself leaning

closer to him. Jake doesn't let on that there's any more tension between us than usual. But the air between us has shifted. It's something closer and vulnerable. Something I should be wary of, but I need it. God, I need it.

I nod once, twisting the little shreds of the napkin I'm destroying in my lap. "I'm who the doctor called." I get choked up again, thinking about how I was listed as his daughter in Henry's phone.

"And Evan?"

"He didn't answer."

Jake backs away from me and seems to question whether or not he wants to respond.

He takes in a heavy breath as if he's going to, but takes a long sip of coffee instead. I watch his face as he stares straight ahead.

"I'm sorry, I shouldn't even be talking about this. I just-"

"Stop saying you're sorry, Kat." Jake turns his head and stares deep into my eyes as he tells me, "You have nothing to be sorry for, and I don't understand why anyone would make you feel like you do."

My breath comes in shorter bursts, my heart beating faster. But all I can think about is how I wish Evan would say those words to me.

My teeth sink into my bottom lip as I reply, "I am sorry though." I don't know what else to say. It's just how I feel.

"Well I'm sorry too. I'm sorry about your father-in-law. And I'm sorry your ex isn't there for you. I'm sure he's going through shit, but it doesn't seem right that he's ignoring you like that. He's got to know it hurts."

"He doesn't feel like my ex most of the time," I admit to Jake with my eyes focused on my fingers as I continue to shred the napkin.

I'm anxious for Jake's response. I just want someone to understand and I feel like Jake can. Even if he can't, I don't think he'll judge me. I hope he won't.

"I mean, you've been married for years, right?" I nod at his question and continue to. "And you only just split?" I nod again to confirm.

"You're going through a lot, and he's not even talking to you. I don't get this guy. I wouldn't throw you away like that."

"I don't think he's throwing me away so much as putting me into a corner while he tries to … " I let out an uneasy sigh.

"I read in the papers about what he's got going on," Jake says and I'm forced to look at him, my heart beating slowly as I wait for his judgment. “I don’t get how the two of you fit together, honestly.”

“We have more in common than you’d think,” I answer him.

“Still have? Or had?” he asks me. And then shakes his head. “Tell me to fuck off if you want,” he says then closes his eyes and takes a quick sip of coffee. “I’m only here if you want to talk. And if I cross a line-”

“You’re not crossing any line,” I tell him and find myself reaching out, letting my hand fall on top of his. Mostly for fear of him backing away and leaving me with nothing again. “I don’t talk to anyone else really.” The plea is unsaid, but Jake hears it.

His eyes assess me and stay on mine as he says, “I don’t want you to get upset with me because of an opinion I have, when I only know a small fraction of the truth. I know the past goes deeper than that.”

It’s small kindnesses that kill the pain. The tiny bits break down walls, making them crumble all because it hits at just the right spot, at just the right time.

“Just don’t hate me for still loving him,” I whisper to him.

“I think you still have feelings for him because you haven’t let anyone else in,” he offers and leans just a bit closer to me.

If Evan would give me just a little, I wouldn't be here. But he won't even text me. It's truly over.

The thought flies through my mind as Jake leans forward a bit more, his gorgeous green eyes focused on my lips.

If Evan would comfort me or let me comfort him, I wouldn't have even called Jake, I think as I close my eyes and breathe in the masculine scent of Jake's cologne. The deep forest fragrance fills my lungs as he gently presses his lips against mine.

If Evan really wanted me, if he cared about me ... the thought is lost as my hands move to Jake's hair, my fingers spearing through it as my mouth parts and Jake deepens the kiss.

The problem is that when my eyes are closed, I picture Evan. It's his fingers that thread through my hair and cup the back of my head. It's his lips pressed against mine.

The problem is when I open my eyes, it's not Evan. No matter how much I want it to be.

DIARY ENTRY 3

HEY MOM,

I REALLY COULD USE you today.

I think Evan hates me maybe. Or he's not the person I thought he was. His father passed away and I went to him. Because I love him even though he's doing all this stupid shit and choosing it over me. But he didn't want me. Not even at the funeral. He hardly looked at me.

Mom, I think he blames me in some way. Or there's something there. I don't understand it. I'm so hurt. I can't describe how it feels because hurt just doesn't do it justice. It's an emptiness I don't know how to fill.

I love him so much, but I just cried alone in the car at the funeral. He didn't hold me. He didn't talk to me. He just hugged me like he hugged everyone else. Like I was no one special.

I thought for a second he would let me cry in his arms. Or that he would cry in my arms like he did when his mom died. But he didn't. He just left.

There's something else too. Something that you might not like. Or I don't know, maybe you'll like it now that you know what Evan did.

I kissed someone else.

I can't help feeling like I'm cheating on Evan.

But if Evan doesn't want me, it's okay, right? It doesn't

feel okay. Separated or divorced, I still love Evan. Even when he treats me like shit.

This guy, his name's Jake, he treats me like he cares about me. Not that we've done anything really. I don't even know him. I think I want to though. And that scares me.

My heart belongs to Evan, but there's someone else who wants to take it.

And seeing Evan at the funeral is what broke me.

I don't know what to do.

I feel like I tell you that a lot. But for the first time, I want to do something. I'm ready for something to change.

CHAPTER 17

Evan

Damn me for what I've done,
Hate me for the lie.
Let the web weave and thread,
But don't let what we have die.

I know it in my blood,
She's mine to keep and hold.
I'll stop fighting only once,
When I'm dead and cold.

The piles of dirt are getting larger. The metal shovels pierce into the frozen soil. The sound cuts through my bones, one and then another and another.

It's been constant as I stand here, helpless. I've never been colder, the wind and bitter snow berating my body, but I still don't move.

I can't take my eyes off of the two graves.

The shovels spill the dirt, mounting the piles as my eyes drift to the tombstones.

The first my father, a man who died before his time. A death of tragedy.

And then to my wife's. My love's. Gone before her time. No one believes me. He put her there. James killed her.

My eyes pop open wide when I hear Kat whisper, "It's all your fault."

I WAKE UP BREATHLESS, my heart pounding and I swear I can feel Kat's hot breath on my neck even though I'm alone. My eyes dart around the room as I slowly pick my body up into a sitting position on the bed.

Just a terror. The same as last night.

I'm quick to grab the video monitor for the security

system off the nightstand and flick the side button on to bring it to life. I had it installed after the break-in.

It's only when I see Kat in our bed that my heart starts to calm and my heated skin seems to succumb to the chill of reality.

She's okay.

I close my eyes and when I open them, it's to a shot of her rolling over in bed. *To my side.* My fingers brush the glass where she is. I'll be there soon. I'll be with her and it'll all be over. I won't let her down.

"THERE'S a lot of shit you aren't going to like," Mason says the second I close the door to his car. He's parked outside of the park and I focus on the people walking by. Moving through their day and carrying on with their lives, while mine's slowly deteriorating into nothing.

I needed this meetup though. I needed to get the fuck out of this rut and talk to someone. Even if it is about this shit.

"Let's start with the easiest," I respond.

"You have a tail. Hired by Lapour," he says and his sentences are short. I nod my head. I figured as much.

I've been scoping James out and James is scoping me out in return. Go figure.

"The cops are coming around your place more often too and they've been poking around your family home, looking through the garbage. A few tags on the station's search engine too."

"They're not going to give up?" I ask with exasperation. This has gone on for too long.

"They just need one thing to pin it on you," Mason says.

"And James has the evidence they'd need to do it." The photos come to mind and my anxiety makes my heart squeeze. I'm waking up to heart palpitations and I'm constantly exhausted but not able to sleep. My leg rocks anxiously from side to side as Mason speaks.

"We can wipe them from his computer, but the hard copies will have to wait till tomorrow. My associate will wipe the place clean, but then he'll know."

"'Bout fucking time."

"It takes time to get a batch of drugs that matches," Mason says defensively. He doesn't get it. It's not his life that's in ruins.

"It would have been easier if we'd found it on him," I tell him.

"Yeah, it would have," he agrees and then it's quiet.

"I feel like I'm failing. All this money paying other people to do shit and we're coming up empty."

"You're doing everything you can."

I can't stand the quiet anymore. "I want this over with," I tell him. A couple days turned into a week. And now the days bleed into one another.

"I'm walking around this city," I tell him, "stalking a man who should be dead. I want to do something!" It's killing me to wait, driving me fucking crazy. I can practically feel my sanity slipping away.

"You have to be careful when you kill someone," he says as if I'm being impatient. "If you're reckless, you get caught."

"Besides, I don't have anything on James. Not a shred of evidence that shows he purchased the strychnine."

"We need evidence and to set him up if there isn't any. Or we can just kill him and end it all." The thought has been pestering the back of my skull. Picking away. I just want to kill the fucker and be done with this.

"You kill him before it's ready and the cops will be looking for his murderer. Is that what you want?"

I know he's right, and I can't answer. I say the only thing that matters, "I need my wife back."

"That's the other thing," he answers while looking out of his window.

"What thing?" I ask staring at him, willing him to look at me. "About my wife?" Adrenaline shoots through me.

"She's seeing someone," he says.

"You're wrong."

"She went out yesterday and we were keeping an eye out. My guys saw some things."

My fists clench at my side as I shake my head. I can already see him. That fucker. Jacob whatever the fuck his last name is. My breathing comes in ragged pants as he says, "Jacob Scott is his name. A potential client of hers."

"Not my wife." I bite it out, although I already know it's true. "She's not going to move on so fast."

The worst part is that I don't even blame her. I'm dying inside. Every night I'm thinking about how my father should still be here and my wife should be in bed with me. Instead I'm alone, clutching a fucking t-shirt Pops always wore. He gave it to me when he gained a little weight and it didn't fit him anymore. It's just a shirt from a shop he used to work at. It's not even around anymore.

I didn't give a shit about it back then, but all I can see when I hold it now is him. It's funny how the little things that don't matter are the most sentimental when you lose the ones you love.

That's my life. Hiding away and mourning my father alone. Hating myself and not being able to fix it all. I can't fix a damn thing.

"I told you she wasn't doing good," Mason says like I should have known better.

My eyes gloss over and I yell at him, "I can't do both at the same time, lead her on that we're broken up but also be there for her." I start pounding my hand against the window like a madman, holding on to the anger and prolonging every other emotion I can until I'm forced to deal with it at night when sleep refuses to comfort me. I know I have to look like I'm fucking unhinged, but I am. So I guess it's fitting. "I can't protect her and have her. There's no way for me to do it!"

"Well if you're not there for her, someone else will be."

My heart's in my throat, that's the only explanation for what I feel. It's not in my chest where it's supposed to be. Only pain is there.

"I want to kill him. That Jacob fuck."

"Now I know that one isn't serious."

"He put his hands on my wife!" I practically spit in his face, but Mason doesn't react.

"She's the one who called him," he says and it guts me.

"What would you do?" I ask him out of desperation as I imagine her calling him. Alone and desperate for someone.

Mason answers with a shrug, "Kill the asshole."

"You're a real wiseass, you know that?" I tell him.

"It could be worse," he says.

"How's that?"

"She cried for a while when she got back from dinner with Jules."

I wait for him to continue, not understanding. "Why was she crying?"

"After seeing the guy, she just cried all night. She's not moving on. She's not okay, Evan."

"What am I supposed to do? She's everything to me. And all I can see, all I dream about at night is her dying because of me." Mason doesn't answer me.

No one has an answer for me. "If I lose her, I have nothing. There's no reason to live if I don't have her."

"You could always go with the locking her in a room option. She likes her office, right?" Mason jokes and I don't know whether to thank him for lightening the mood or punch his fucking face in.

"Do you think James would go after her if I took her back?" I ask him. "Tell me honestly."

"If someone wanted to hurt you, the first thing they'd do is go after her," Mason says exactly what I feel and I rest my head against the window. It feels like I'm dying inside. There's only so much pain a person can handle.

"He still might, but the chance of that seems low. Right now James is only interested in three people: you, Samantha and a man named Andrew Jones. Obviously a cover."

Before I can ask, Mason adds, "We're paying him a visit soon. Just trying to track down his location."

I nod my head, but all I can think about is that prick with his hands on my wife.

"What if we paid Jacob a visit?"

"You really think that's the way to go? Like Kat won't find out?" he asks me and I grind my teeth.

"What if she goes home? What if you go home? Just be

quiet about it. Rent a hotel room and make sure you're seen there for your tail. But go to her at night and make sure she keeps quiet."

"My wife can't keep a secret for shit."

"She's talking about going back home anyway. You're going to need to be there."

"You think she'd be cool with me just slipping in at night? Maybe if I told her what's going on. But in and out, just coming and going as I please? She'd kill me."

"Don't tell her shit. Are you fucking crazy?" he asks me.

"Lie to her?" I ask him. Kat's always been able to see right through me.

"I'm not saying lie to her. I'm just saying this is how it has to be. And right now she needs comfort."

"James thinks you're with Samantha, so be seen with her, then head over to your place."

"You want my wife to hate me?" I ask him.

"It's the only real option you have right now," he says and looks me in the eyes to add, "She'll never know."

CHAPTER 18

Kat

Hate creeps slowly,
Drifting in my veins.
So silent, so lethal,
Locking me in chains.
My vision turning red,
My blood pumping hard.
You're the reason I can't forgive,
You're the reason my heart is scarred.

I HAVE to tell Evan about Jake, but he doesn't want to talk to me.

He's ignoring me. Intentionally hurting me.

Yet, there's still a sense of obligation. As if I owe it to him to let him know that I'm moving on now. Like I've finally got a grip on my self-respect, but I need him to know it. I roll my eyes at the thought and heave out an aggravated sigh.

I don't care if it's weak or pathetic. He was everything to me.

I nearly trip as I realize what I thought. *Was.*

Is it really over? I struggle to breathe in the cold air as I think maybe a small part of me wants to move on. No, that's not it. It's simply accepting that it's time to move on.

Say something, I'm giving up on you … song lyrics play through my head as my throat dries and I force myself to keep walking up the sidewalk to 82 Brookside. Evan's family home.

The soft lyrics of the sad song are what keep me from knocking on his door at first. I try to compose myself because if Evan doesn't open this door, or worse, he does but doesn't hear me out? Then I have no hope left.

I know deep down in my gut, this is my last and final effort.

Say something, I'm giving up on you … and then the soundtrack stops, a feminine voice cutting through. The voice of a woman I know.

Samantha.

I hear her laugh and then a muted voice. His voice. She's in there with him.

I thought my heart was already broken. Apparently it was only torn, because at this moment, there's no denying my heart's been ripped ruthlessly in half.

I'm numb as I stand in the harsh cold, trying to listen to the faint sounds as I lean my body toward the window to my right. I can barely see her and I can't see him at all.

There's no way I can make out what they're saying, but I watch her put on her coat.

It's funny how anger can so easily replace sadness. Almost like rock-paper-scissors. Anger beats sadness, sadness beats … I don't know what and in this moment, I don't give a fuck.

My heartbeat picks up; my breathing gets shallow as I watch that bitch standing in Evan's parents' home.

What a fucking fool I was.

Of course this is why he left me. My breathing falters as I take a few steps back from the door, shoving my hair out of my face and trying to collect myself.

I hug myself as I walk aimlessly down the street. My shoes crunch the thin layer of fallen snow beneath my feet as I get farther and farther away. I let my mind whirl and my emotions stir into a concoction of self-doubt and recklessness.

"He thought I would wait for him while he had one last fling?" I whisper beneath my breath but then shake my head. "Maybe he's trying to pick which one of us he wants ... "

Like a madwoman I talk to myself, ignoring the honking horns and cars speeding down the street next to me. I let out a sarcastic laugh and think, *his choice is made.*

He already left me and I already told him it was over.

How fucking dumb can I really be?

My hands fumble inside of my jacket as I round the street corner. I bite down on the cloth of my glove and pull it off so I can unlock my phone.

Evan's cheating on me. I text Jules first. I've talked to her more than anyone else since she's welcomed me into her house.

No, he can't be! She's quick to text back and I find myself standing still in the middle of the busy sidewalk, texting her back. Everyone walks around me, ignoring me and my mental breakdown.

I'm pregnant with his child and he's cheating on me.

Why would you think that? she texts back as I type my response.

I just saw her.

Saw who? she asks.

Samantha

And they were kissing??? That bastard!!

I bite the inside of my cheek and hate that I can't say yes they were kissing. Samantha's the fucking enemy and she's inside his house. Isn't that enough?

I didn't see them kiss. She's in his house though.

What were they doing? she asks me and I find my anger turning on her.

I don't know!

What were you doing, spying??

OMG Jules! YES of course I was! I stand there numb, reading the text messages and feeling like I truly am crazy.

What did he say? she asks me.

About them? I didn't go in, I text her. I stand there for a moment with no response back. The wind seems to pick up and my ears burn from the cold. Or maybe from people talking about me.

I'm going to get proof. I text Jules back and spin around on my heels, shoving the phone into my coat pocket and ignoring the dings of her return messages.

I'll confront that bastard and make him pay for the hell he's put me through. All the while I work myself up. Each step back to his house is taken with strong and stronger resolution.

But his car's not there and just like my gut told me the second I saw the spot empty in front of his house, the door is locked.

"Motherfucker," I scream out as I bang my fists against the door. The chill in the air makes each impact hurt more and more.

I start to text him even though my hands are aching and freezing cold. One line saying, *I know.* And then I back out. Fuck that, it's too mysterious. I text him a paragraph about what I saw, but I delete that too, knowing he'll just deny it.

I stand there outside of his parents' house. Outside of the house that I fell in love with him in. And I slip my phone in my pocket.

I'm not going to text him, or confront him. Nothing. I'll

figure out the truth and make sure I have evidence, but I'm giving Evan exactly what he gave me … nothing.

Diary Entry 4

Mom,

I'm worried about the things that I think sometimes.

I'm worried about how angry I get. Did you get like that ever?

I don't know if you would have. I feel like I did it to myself by marrying Evan.

I'm filled with anger more than anything. I don't want to be like this, but it's what he's done to me. Maybe that's an excuse … that's probably what you'd tell me, isn't it?

I've never been this angry and I'm afraid of what I'm going to do.

I'm trying so hard to be strong, but what is strength when you have no control?

I need to take it back. Whether Evan likes it or not.

CHAPTER 19

Evan

Bitter cold will greet me,
For what I've kept from you.
The chill freezing inch by inch,
And making my skin turn blue.
It's meant as punishment,
Maybe to kill me too.
But what you cannot know,
Is that it's always been for you.

I HAVEN'T BEEN this nervous since Kat and I first went out on a date.

We were just going to the club. *My* club. I didn't own it;

never got into commercial real estate, although I have thought about it. It was still my club though. At least that's how I felt. And I should've felt in control and powerful to meet her in front of the doors, the music drifting out into the street.

But one look at her stepping out of her car had my heart pumping faster and the back of my neck sweating.

Kat's always been able to stun me like that.

As if I don't already know she's beautiful.

It's something else though.

The feeling that I can't hold on to her. That's the feeling I had flowing in my veins that night, and that's the feeling now as I get ready to step up to the doors of Mason's house in the Berkshires.

I check my phone again to see if I have any more texts from him, but I don't. The last one said she was packing her stuff and planning on moving back to the townhouse.

Short stay for her, and Jules is crushed, but she just wants to be alone.

Kat says that a lot, but I know her. She doesn't want to be alone.

I rap the back of my knuckles on the hard oak doors, the cold air making it hurt just a bit. My body urges me to do it harder, to feel the pain and focus on that and not the anxiety of rejection.

I would deserve it, after all.

The door opens in one tug, and the glow of the foyer chandelier flows to the porch. There she is. Holding the door open with her lips parted in shock.

"Evan," she says my name as she stands perfectly still.

A faint dusting of snow settles around me as I take her in. From the white socks on her feet, to the silk pajamas that must be a gift from Jules, 'cause I've never seen them before in my life.

"Hey," I say and then swallow the lump in my throat. "I heard you were here."

Her expression hardens instantly as she seems to get over my surprise arrival.

"What do you want?" she asks me and then starts to come outside rather than letting me in, like a fucking lunatic.

"What are you doing?" I ask her with complete disbelief as she tries to shut the door.

"I'm not having this conversation in Jules' house," Kat spits out like I'm the one who's lost their mind.

"Baby, get inside, it's freezing out!"

"Don't tell me what to do!" she yells back at me and it's like being struck across the face. I take it though. I take one step back and watch as she crosses her arms over her chest and her cheeks slowly turn pink from the wind that won't let up. "What do you want?"

"Are you sure you don't want to go inside?" I ask her as calmly as I can, trying to be reasonable.

"I went to your house today," she says and I can feel the blood drain from my face.

"Is that right?" I ask her, my body tensing up. All I can hear is my heart pounding as I feel her slipping away from me.

"I don't want anything to do with you, Evan," she tells me with a cracked voice. At least there's emotion left. If there's that, then I still have a chance.

"I don't know what you think you saw," I start to tell her and then flinch from her shriek.

"Think!" she yells. "I saw her!" She moves in closer, getting in my face to scream at me. "Samantha. You left me to be with her," she seethes, the accusation coming out hard.

"You see me touch her?" I ask her, taking a step closer to her. "I know you didn't, 'cause I never would."

"She was with you," she breathes out her words with nothing but pain and agony.

"Yeah, she was. A few times in the last week," I confess to her. I don't want her to find out any other way. "I'm trying to fix things and she's-"

"I want you to go," she says.

"I won't until you tell me you believe me." I look her in the eyes and wait for it.

"Just go!"

"Never. I would never stray from you." As I say the words, it's crippling. Because I know she did what she's accusing me of. She's the one who's seeing someone else, but I gave her the space to do it. I left her side.

She doesn't answer me, merely shivers in the cold as her bottom lip starts to turn blue.

"Let's go inside," I urge her, but she doesn't respond. "I want to talk."

"I thought the funeral might be a good time to talk," she finally says with tears in her eyes. "Guess you didn't?

Her words slice through me, down to my core. "It meant a lot to me that you were there," I manage to say, but I can't look her in the eyes.

"Didn't seem like it," she replies, although she's lost a bit of strength in her voice.

"I'm having a difficult time handling it," I tell her, scrambling for an excuse, but there's so much truth in those words.

James was there at the funeral. He even shook my hand, the fucking bastard. The reason is right there on the tip of my tongue. I wanted to go to her, to hold her. To go home with her and get lost in her love. More than anything.

"You think it was easy for me?" she asks me after a moment of silence.

"You think it was easy for me?" I shoot right back and the memories of the grave, the service hit me. I have to pinch the bridge of my nose and close my eyes as I see the visions of the nightmares mixing with the memories. *I shouldn't even be here.* Regret flows through my veins. What am I doing?

"I'm sorry," she whispers and her breath turns to fog. The wind blows and her hair falls in front of her face as I tell her, "I'm sorry too." I get a little choked up, but I manage to tell her, "He loved you so much."

He really did. His voice telling me to make it right won't shut up in my head and it kills my strength.

"I told you I just needed time." I try to make the words come out strong, but all it is, is a plea. I don't know what to do anymore.

All I want to do is protect her. *Maybe that means losing her forever.*

She shakes her head. "What part of us moving on with our lives and doing it together didn't you understand? I don't have time for games or whatever trouble you've gotten into."

"I'm fixing the trouble." I refuse to give up. "I just need more time."

"And how much longer is that going to be? How much longer do I have to sit on the back burner and wait for you to love me again?"

"I still love you," I say.

"You don't act like it."

"There's a reason for everything, I promise." I have to blink away the scenes of the funeral, of the night terrors.

"I don't even want to hear your excuses anymore," she says and wipes under her eyes. She sounds so defeated. "You're supposed to be here for me."

I question everything in that moment. I'm so afraid of losing her, but the image of her dead on the ground makes me harden my resolve. So I hesitate and immediately regret it.

"I need you to go, Evan. For good."

"It's 'cause of Jacob, isn't it?" I can't help but blurt it out. I want someone else to blame. Someone else to hate other than myself. "You're moving on with him?"

I can't help but point out that she's the one who wants something else. I only want her. I won't lose her. I'll fuck her so good, until she forgets any other man exists.

"You think I need a man? You think I need someone?" Her voice is coated in an anger I haven't seen from her before. "I never needed anyone! You're the only one I ever let in. I even kept away your father. You were the only one I let get close and I'll be fine, living the rest of my life alone."

"You want him more than me?" My jealousy gets the best of me.

"Get away from me!" she spits out as she opens the door to get into the house.

"I'm coming back for you," I tell her and I mean it.

"Well I won't be here, and I'm changing the locks on the townhouse. So good fucking luck with that."

CHAPTER 20

Kat

So many stories deep inside,
So many stories, secrets to hide.
Just keep it quiet, you must plead,
They string you along and make you bleed.
A clean slate, tainted with the past,
You knew this would never last.
Just do your best to make amends,
But this is not where your story ends.

It's the heavy pit in your stomach. It rocks back and forth, making you queasy and your body can't sit still.

That's what it feels like when you know you're about to hurt someone.

At least that's how it feels right now.

I don't need anyone at all. And I don't want anyone either. Maybe I'm proving it to myself, or maybe to Evan. I don't care which.

My pulse quickens and I try to swallow the spiked ball in my throat when I hear the bell at the front of the café.

Jacob smiles so sweetly, with genuine happiness and he strolls over to the table, letting his jacket slip off his shoulders. I'm going to miss this. The comfort his presence brings.

"One more nice day before winter comes in," he says easily.

"Got that for you," I say, nodding my head to the ceramic mug on the table. I have to force the smile to stay on my face, but it doesn't fool Jacob.

"What's wrong?" he asks me, not touching the mug.

I hate that I get choked up. It's stupid really.

It was just friends, then just a kiss.

But it never should have been anything.

I shake my head slightly, and pick up the mug. Jake's face falls, but he still tries to cheer me up.

"So I never got your answer about the movies tomorrow night," he says with a kind smile. "I heard it's going to be good."

My mug clinks on the small plate as he adds, "I love coffee shops and all, but it'd be nice to do something more."

More.

It would be. I can see it. I can feel it. If my heart didn't belong to someone else, I could see Jacob being so much more.

"I have to tell you something." I let the words out before I change my mind and swallow them. Before I give in to getting over Evan by getting under another man.

Jacob visibly winces and then scratches the side of his neck as he looks to the right. "That doesn't sound so good."

"I kind of lied to you," I tell him, feeling a vise grip around my heart.

"You're not separated?" he assumes.

"No, we are. But I don't want to be," I blurt out.

"You still love him. I know you do." I nod at his words.

"There's more," I say and hesitate.

"Just tell me," he says, moving his hand to mine and I stare down at where his skin touches mine. It's gentle, kind. It's the comfort I desperately need. But I can't be expected to always have someone to lean on. I want to stand on my own.

"I'm pregnant," I tell him and the only reaction I get is that his brow raises just slightly. It's comical really, and the small movement makes me smile slightly.

"*That,* I didn't see coming," he says, keeping a small bit of humor in his voice. He slowly pulls his hand away, but keeps it on the tabletop. I notice the absence instantly though.

"Not far along?"

I shake my head no at his question. "How long have you known?" he asks me and it makes my heart drop.

"A while," I answer.

"So that's the lie?"

"Yeah," I answer. "I'm sorry."

"Don't be," he tells me as if it's no big deal.

"I knew better, it was just ... " I trail off and swallow my words, staring at a stain on the table. One that will never go away.

"It was nice being *okay* with someone?" he asks me and I chance a peek up into his eyes. There's nothing but understanding there.

"Yeah," I answer him and chew on my bottom lip. "I just wanted to pretend to be okay for a little bit."

"Well it's not pretend," he tells me and adjusts in his seat. "You can be okay if you want to." It's hard to hold his gaze as he brings his hand back to mine.

"Does he know?" he asks me and I can only nod.

"And he … ?" he starts to ask, but doesn't finish the obvious question.

"Says he's happy but he's still not with me. He's not committing and carrying on like he was. I want him, but I need him with me and he's not…" I'm ashamed of the answer.

It's quiet for a short moment.

"So … do you want to go to the movies?" Jacob asks and then picks up his mug. "I'd still like to go if you would," he says.

My heart does this little flutter, a quick flicker of warmth that lets me know it's still there. It's in gratitude and I think that's all I could give anyone else. It's all I'm willing to do.

I shake my head no and give him a sad smile.

"Well, I had to ask. 'Cause I think it would have been good," he tells me, forcing a smile and then covering his disappointment by taking a large sip of the chai.

"You going to be okay?" he asks me.

I shrug, honestly unsure of whether or not I'll ever be okay. "Some people are meant to be alone." *Or waiting on a love that may never come back.*

"You sound like me," he says and takes a deep, heavy breath. "Gets tiresome though."

"A story for another time perhaps?"

"I think it's the same story mostly, with only one big difference."

"What's that?" I ask.

"I think Evan may love you back, just like you love him. Whether or not he deserves it ... well that's a matter of opinion, I guess." I can't respond and instead I let my gaze wander back to the stain. "It wasn't the same for me. It was only one-sided."

"I'm so sorry, Jake." It's all I can tell him and I genuinely am.

"Don't be," he says easily. "Fate puts people in our life for a reason." He takes a steadying breath before saying, "And now I know it's possible."

"What's possible?" For a moment I worry that he thinks the two of us being together is still an option, when it's not at all for me.

"Not this like you and me," he says, hearing my unspoken thought. "Trust me, I wish it were. But I meant … just that there could be someone else for me."

"You could always write the story. Although I doubt you'd want me to be your agent, huh?"

"No agent," he says with the same sad smile on his face that I've been giving him.

"Maybe we could still be friends?" I offer.

"I don't think that's for the best, Kat. I can't just be friends with you."

My hair tickles my shoulders as I nod and reach for my coat to leave. My movements are sluggish; I don't want this to be the last goodbye. But it is. And I know it. I barely touched my drink and didn't have anything to eat, but that's okay. I knew I wouldn't anyway.

"How about this," Jacob offers as I pull my wool coat tight around my shoulders. "You call me. If you're ever not okay and want more. But I won't call you or text you again. It's in your hands."

"I'm sorry, Jake." I say the words, but they don't even make a dent in expressing what I feel.

"Stop being sorry. Do that one thing for me, will you?" he asks and I merely nod and say my goodbye.

Every step back to my townhouse, I wanted to go back.

Every breath, I wished I could tell him that what he did for me, I could never repay and I'll be forever thankful for that.

But neither of those things happened. I walked back to my townhouse alone and the first thing I did when I got home was to delete his emails and his number.

I didn't want to have the option to run back to him.

Jacob is a good man. But he's not for me. I don't need someone else to love me. I need to learn to love being alone again. That's what I need, 'cause then I'm forced to love myself.

Diary Entry 5

Dear Mom,

It's not so bad being alone.

I remember thinking that same thought a while after you guys left me. I know it's not your fault.

I just can't stand to think of needing someone. Not when it hurts so freaking bad when they leave you. Did you see what Evan did? I gave him that power. And that's my fault. I won't do it again.

I should have known better.

If you could just remind me, maybe? The next time he comes around and says he wants me and that he loves me, can you give me a sign? Something that will remind me that he's just going to hurt me.

People don't change and some people are meant to be alone.

I promise I'll be okay from now on, Mom.

I just forgot that I'm one of those people. But I remember now. I won't forget again.

CHAPTER 21

Evan

Secrets make cracks so deep,
Loving the crumbling walls.
Temptation hiding deep within,
Hissing as it crawls.

It wants to burrow deep inside,
Warming your beating heart.
It carves into your very soul,
A promise never to leave, a threat never to part.

I'M USED to sneaking around. I've done it all my life. I guess you could say I'm a fucking professional at it.

The door to the townhouse opens and I turn to look over my shoulder. No one knows I'm here. And I need to keep it that way.

The pictures of my wife and I stare back at me as I slowly close the door. Feeling the warmth and familiarity of the home I built with Kat makes the ache deep in my chest twist and turn to a sickening degree.

The large clock on the back wall ticks loudly as I move through the place. It's nearly 3 a.m., but I needed to make sure I wasn't being followed.

The life I led destroyed the only thing I ever had that I wanted to keep. My marriage.

I haven't told her the truth, and I can't. The knowledge pushes me forward, each step bringing me closer to her. Closer to the bed we once shared, and closer to her warmth under the covers. As I push the door open, my heart beats slow. Every second making my skin heat and the worry threatening to consume me.

But the sight of her steady breathing and the faint movements of her body as she stirs in her sleep put all my worries behind me. She's safe, and that's what matters.

Her eyes flutter open and I stand as still as can be, terrified that she'll see, but she merely turns, pulling the thin white sheet with her.

The moonlight filters in through the curtains and leaves a trail of shadows that accentuate her curves as they play across the bed. She's still as gorgeous as ever. Even in her sleep with no makeup on and her bare skin kissed by the faint light of the early morning, she holds a beauty that no one will surpass for me.

How many nights passed with me failing to see that? How much time have I wasted?

I can't let a soul know I still love her. They'll use her to get back at me.

My eyes widen and my grip tightens on the door as I hear my name slip through her lips. "Evan." It sounded like a prayer, or maybe a plea. A soft moan escapes her lips as I take a hesitant step forward, wondering if she saw me or if I'm only with her in her dreams.

I start to question if she even said it, but then she says it again. The sweet sound of her soft cadence whispering my name is everything I need to keep going.

I swallow thickly, hating myself for what I've done and what I've put her through.

CHAPTER 22

Kat

It's a feeling of unworthiness,
Undeserving of his trust.
That's the part that kills my heart,
And turns my lust to dust.
My body begs me to fight for him,
To prove to him he's wrong.
But he's the one who should cave,
And I've known that all along.

My eyes pop open at the familiar creak from the stairs. My heart races faster and faster as I lie as still as I can. My body's hot and the covers are making me even hotter, but I don't move. I try not to even breathe as I wait for another sound. But nothing comes.

It's just my nerves. Maybe a nightmare.

Slowly, my breath comes back, but I'm still too scared to move nonetheless. I blink away the sleep and tilt my head just enough to look at the clock on my nightstand. 04:14 AM stares back at me in bright red digital numbers.

The sounds of the city streets filter in and my heartbeat fades. It was nothing, I whisper and reach for my glass of water, downing it and then wishing there was more.

Get up.

I will my body to move. I wince and crack my back, letting my bare feet hit the cold hardwood floor. I don't like sleeping alone and I don't like how Evan's side of the bed doesn't have that faint smell of his anymore. I can feel the solemn expression on my face as I glance at where he used to sleep, but I keep going.

The floor protests as I walk, and I let the feeling that someone was in here leave me. I need a security system … or a dog. A big dog.

The corners of my lips tip up into a smile as I walk down the stairs.

Pushing back the hair from my face, I walk to the kitchen

and turn on the light. It's so early, but I'm hungry. To sleep, or not to sleep becomes the question.

It only takes a glass of water, two Twinkies and a couple handfuls of grapes before I don't feel so hungry anymore and sleep is calling me upstairs again.

Passing through the dining room, I check over my shoulder, just to make sure there's no one here. That eerie feeling is still clinging to me.

I think I'll name the dog Brutus. My lips purse as I wonder how dogs do with infants ... I make a mental note to look that up first thing tomorrow.

I think I'm starting to really feel pregnant. It's beyond being exhausted. It's something else.

I almost head back upstairs, but my eyes catch sight of the flowers on the table.

The flowers Jacob sent me when Henry died are already wilted. Bright yellow sunflowers. They're large and the stems are thick. But they'll eventually die and by the looks of them, it'll be soon. That's what flowers do. They die.

Next to the vase is my laptop and I absently pull it toward the edge of the table and take a seat. My body aches, my hips especially, and sitting up feels better than lying down. I might as well get a little work in before I try to sleep again.

A yawn leaves me as the dim light of the computer brightens.

Studying the flowers again, I think about how fucked up it is that I turned down a man who could have been perfect for me. My fingertips brush along the petals. I'll never know, but I don't want to lean on a man or anyone else.

It's time I took control of my life.

My to-do list is already set. First step: I need a new place. Somewhere near the Manhattan Bridge, I think. I click my laptop on and check my messages and emails, simply out of habit. But I'm so tired. A few of the candidates I picked to interview to be my personal assistant emailed me back. There are two of them I really like. I might actually hire both of them. Maybe that's really step one. And then finding the perfect place will be step two. A smile plays across my lips and I nod to myself in agreement of my early morning can't sleep, aha moment.

It feels good that I've got a plan to focus on. I rest my hand on my belly. And I'll have it all fixed and ready before this one gets here. He or she will never know this place or all the hell that went on here.

My eyes drift across the room and the night that started it all plays out in front of my eyes. I look at the head chair and envision myself sitting there like a ghost, drinking wine and wanting to deny it and at the same time hating Evan because I knew he was lying.

A dreadful breath leaves me and a sadness weighs down on my chest, but there's conviction there too.

A new place, a new way of life. My fingers drift to my belly button and then lower. A new life entirely.

Diary Entry 6

Hey Mom, can I take back what I said?

I don't think alone is the right word. Alone hurts my heart a lot. It hurts more than I want to admit. Mom, it feels like the worst thing in the world.

I think that's why I clung to Jake. I just didn't want to be alone.

But more than that, I want to be loved by someone who can love me the way I need.

I think maybe he could love me. It's just not the right kind of love.

How did you know Dad loved you the way you needed? I just laughed a little writing this. I'm sure he made it obvious. He didn't hurt you like Evan does to me.

I hope it doesn't make you mad. I don't think he means it. I just think he doesn't know any better.

But I want more, Mom. I really want someone to love me.

I want them to love me like Evan used to love me.

I don't know if it's possible. I don't know if maybe something's wrong with me.

No, scratch that, there's definitely something wrong with me.

I'm going to find someone.

Maybe not now, I don't know when. And I'm not going to use them or compare them to Evan. It'll take time, but I think eventually I'll be able to do this.

You know sometimes I hate myself? Maybe that's why no one can love me right. I can't even love myself right.

But this baby makes me feel loved. This baby will love me, won't he?

I promise I'll give him every bit of love I have. I hope it's enough.

CHAPTER 23

Evan

To move the mountains would be weak,
In comparison to what I'll do.
There's nothing that could hold me back,
You know I'd kill for you.
The danger that comes with it,
The sins that lie ahead.
It's the only thing that keeps me from you,
But losing you is what I dread.

SHE TOOK off her ring today.

I watched on a fucking security monitor as she slipped it

off and held it between her fingers. Miles away with the sins of the city between us, all I could do was watch.

I shift my weight to my left leg, slowly as I quietly open the door.

Kat didn't change the locks like she threatened to do, but that wouldn't have stopped me anyway.

This is the point that I've truly gone crazy, but losing the woman you love will do that to a man. Watching her walk away when you know she loves you and you love her; it's a torture that's immeasurable and the destruction it leaves is unforgivable.

One step in, and not the faintest of sounds. The front door to the townhouse closes behind me softly.

Maybe I should have called, maybe I should have announced myself, but it's my home. She's my wife and this is where I belong.

I can accept that now. If I can keep secrets, so can Kat. I swallow thickly, closing my eyes and hating myself as I lock the front door. *She better be able to.*

I'm a desperate man. If anything happens to her, I'll end it. I already know that. But I'm so fucking weak that I'm risking it. If only she can keep a secret, we'll be alright.

My eyes open at the sound of the microwave beeping in the kitchen.

Beep, beep, beep and then I hear the door open.

She's so close and knowing what I'm about to do, my heart races and I find it hard to swallow.

My body doesn't wait for me. My feet move on their own, pushing me closer to her. I need to see her, even if she doesn't see me. I can't explain why, it just needs to be in person.

The only light in the townhouse that's on is the kitchen light. It's early morning and I wasn't planning on her being awake.

I was just going to leave the gift on her nightstand. Maybe it's a sign that she's awake. A sign that I can't be a coward any longer.

That's what a man who waits in the shadows is. That's what a man who hurts his wife is.

I walk into the kitchen expecting her to see me, but her back is turned as she stirs something in a bowl and then pops it into the microwave.

Fuck, I've missed this view. When she raises her arms, the t-shirt she has on slips up past her thighs and gives me the smallest peek of her ass.

I almost groan from primal deprivation. It feels like forever since I've held her, laid her in bed and enjoyed her in every way possible.

"Kat," I say her name softly as the microwave starts and she whips around, backing into the cabinets with her hand on her chest.

I can see the outline of her breasts through the shirt and with her dark brunette hair a mess from sleep, she's never looked more beautiful. More fuckable.

"You scared the shit out of me," Kat says after a second, breathless.

"I'm sorry," I tell her. "I didn't mean to." I take a chance to move closer, but stop at the kitchen counter.

"What are you doing here?" she asks. The microwave beeps and she rips the door open without even looking and then slams it shut.

I cock a brow at her anger, but she doesn't react.

"I brought these," I tell her and pull the pair of baby shoes from my jacket pocket. They're the same pair I wore when I was little. Smooth leather and simple, but before me, they were my father's. I found them in a box in Pops' basement.

Kat pinches the bridge of her nose and turns her shoulder to me, hiding her expression.

"Baby?" I whisper softly, cautiously even.

"What are you doing?" she asks me and looks me in the eyes.

"I know you're angry."

"Angry doesn't even begin to cut it."

"I know you'll forgive me too," I tell her with feigned confidence. I fucking hope she will. But from the look on her face, she knows it's a bluff as much as I do.

"Fuck off," she spits out.

"Because you love me. And you know I love you."

"You love me?" she asks angrily. She storms toward me, sticking her finger in my chest as she yells. "This is what love is?" She shoves me back and I take it, loving the fight in her. But it doesn't last long.

"Your father died and I had to be alone," she speaks lowly and then takes a step back. "You chose to be alone," she whispers. She tries turning from me again, but I grip her wrist.

"I didn't want it to be like that. I swear to you." Bringing up my Pops hits me hard. I keep forgetting. And that's how I want it to be. I keep thinking he'll call or text. I keep thinking when all this is over, we'll have dinner together on Sundays again. And I hate it when I remember he's not here anymore.

"I'm sorry," I tell her as the feeling of worthlessness washes over me.

"Sorry doesn't cut it!" she screams at me, her face turning red.

"You know what loving you means?" I ask her, raising my voice. "It means protecting you."

"You can take all those words and-"

"They're in my vows," I heave out the words, my emotions rising and the thought of losing Kat forever becoming more and more real. "Protecting you is in my vows."

"Don't talk to me about vows," she spits out. I've never seen her so angry. The look in her eyes is pure hate.

"Come here," I tell her and her eyes narrow.

She tilts her head to the side and looks at me as if I've lost my mind. My heart feels like it does a somersault, a painful flip in my chest as she says, "Don't tell me what to do."

"The only reason I've been gone is because being seen

with you would put you in danger." I hate myself the moment the confession slips out. Weak. I'm so fucking weak. I need to be a better man for her, but I've never been good enough and we both know that.

Kat's silent, but her expression is unchanged.

"I had to do it."

"You don't have to do a damn thing but breathe," she says, leaning forward and gripping onto the counter behind her. It's as if clinging to the counter is the only thing keeping her from clawing my eyes out.

"I was only trying to keep you safe," I say the words lowly as the sight of Kat in front of me becomes more of a reality than my fear ever was.

She hates me. I've made my wife hate me.

"Well thank you for that," she says sarcastically with tears in her eyes.

"I swear." I feel tears prick my eyes as I fall to my knees in front of her. "I'm only here right now because I can't stay away any longer." My heart crumples at the words that I choke on.

Kat takes a small step back, brushing against the counter as she does and I grip on to her, begging her to listen.

"I didn't know it would take this long."

"What would?" she asks me, crossing her arms and refusing to look in my eyes, but she's full of emotion and on edge waiting for me to open up to her. That's what made her fall in love with me. I swallow the thick lump in my throat and pray that I'm not making a mistake.

"I'm ... " I can hardly breathe as the words *threatening, investigating, framing* get caught in my throat.

"Tell me, Evan." Kat licks her lower lip and stares down at me with tired eyes. "I've had enough and I'm over the secrets and the lies. I'm over this," she says and gestures between us although as she does, her expression morphs into pain.

"It's going to sound crazy," I warn her.

"I'm already there," she answers me sarcastically.

"James is the one who's responsible for Tony's death," I tell her, still on my knees although I let go of her. I hate myself for telling her and bringing her into this, and I almost don't say another word. I slowly rise to my feet and Kat takes a step forward.

"You better tell me," she hisses, grabbing the arm of my jacket and forcing me to look at her.

"He was trying to kill me." My throat feels dry and scratchy as the words slowly leave me. "And he knows I know."

Kat shakes her head. It's a small motion of disbelief, but she doesn't speak as she drops her arm.

"It's because of his divorce. He wants Samantha scared and he wanted to prove he'd do anything."

Her mouth opens and closes, but she still says nothing.

Please believe me. "We've been tracking his schedule and routines, breaking into his house and office looking for evidence or something that can prove it."

A huff of disbelief so faint I almost think I imagine it leaves Kat's lips as she turns from me, facing the sink and putting her fingers to her lips.

"Talk to me, please," I beg her and a trace of anger flashes in her eyes.

"You could have gone to the cops," she finally says. "Like a normal human being."

"I couldn't go to the cops with nothing on him and James has proof. It's his word against mine and he has photos."

"He has photos of what, exactly?" she asks me.

"I was with Tony the night he died. James has pictures. He tried blackmailing me-"

"Jesus Christ," Kat exclaims.

"You see why I didn't tell you? It's too much and you're

pregnant. If he's after me and he knows I love you, he'd go after you too."

"You could have messaged me; you didn't have to hurt me."

"He's tracking my texts, babe, he's following my every step. Just to get here, I had to make sure to lose the guy he paid to follow me around."

"This is insane, Evan. You know that, don't you?" She shakes her head again.

"I know, and I'm sorry. I have someone working on it and we're trying."

"Who?" she asks immediately and when I don't answer she adds, "No more secrets, and no more lies. I want all of it."

"Mason," I tell her and it takes a moment to register.

"Does Jules know?" she asks me.

"I doubt it," I answer her.

"So because you think I could have been in potential danger, you left me alone, treated me like shit and tortured me?"

"He would have killed you," I tell her, stressing the truth of the situation.

"You don't know that!" she shrieks at me.

"I met him and he brought you up," my throat goes dry at the memory. "He would have gone for you Kat.

She shakes her head in disbelieving motions.

"If I lose you, I have nothing!" The words rip up from my throat, desperate for her to see what I've been seeing. To feel what I've been feeling. Complete and utter loss. I calm my voice and take a step closer to her and say, "If he killed you, I would have nothing to live for."

She stares into my eyes with a look I can't place and says, "I'd rather die beside you, than live without you."

"I would kill myself if anyone hurt you. I don't know how you can't see that." She appraises me for a moment, calming down slightly but still taking in everything I've confessed. "I promise it's almost over. I promise I wouldn't do this if I didn't have to."

"You should have known better than to keep that from me. What if you had died?" she asks me and I can't answer right away. I'd never considered it.

"I was only planning to keep you safe; I wasn't concerned for myself," I finally answer.

Her face scrunches in complete disapproval.

"How dare you," she says and condemns my actions.

"If you do what I say, we can still be together," I tell her and the reaction I get is nothing like what I'd planned. She's not at all moved by my confession. She can't tell a soul or let on that we're together. "If we're together," I stop mid-sentence, afraid that we're not. Afraid that it's too late.

"You don't control me," she seethes.

"Kat, I love you, but I will lock you in a fucking room to keep you safe. If you don't listen to me, then you leave me with no choice. I swear to God I will."

Smack!

My face burns with a stinging sensation as the sound rings in the air. My heart stops beating as my eyes widen, taking in the vision of a pissed off Kat in front of me with her hand still raised. My hand slowly rises to my jaw.

I've never seen Kat strike a person in my life. She's not a violent person by nature.

But I guess I had it coming to me.

"Don't you dare tell me that you love me."

"I love you more than anything, and I'll never deny it. I'll tell you every single day for the rest of my life."

"Really? 'Cause you haven't said a word to me in weeks!

I'm pregnant with your child. A baby, Evan. And you left me. You left *us*."

"I just told you why," I point out. "I never really left you, Kat, and you know that."

"You wanted me to believe that you had, and that's even worse," she says and I'm taken aback.

"You wanted me to hurt," she says with spite.

"No," I pipe up but she keeps going, shoving her hands into my chest.

"You wanted me to cry every night, knowing I wasn't worth your time anymore."

"That's not true," I tell her as tears prick my eyes.

"You could have told me the truth and not just that you were leaving for a short while and then ignore me."

"I couldn't risk you slipping."

"I can keep a secret too."

"One slip is all it will take. If anyone even thinks we're back together… that's all it would take."

"Well you told me now," she says with finality and I take her hand in mine, forcing it up so she can see.

"Because you took off your ring," I tell her, not holding

back the pain it caused. "Because you kissed someone else." Her fight vanishes, not all at once, but slowly as both of us breathe heavily, the air between us getting hotter. "Because I thought I was losing you forever."

"You left me with no choice," she tells me although a look of regret flashes in her eyes.

"I didn't have one either. You have to believe me."

"You love me?" she asks me.

"I do. You have to know it's true. I know you do."

"You want to be with me? You want to keep me yours?" she asks, completely serious.

"Yes, it's all I want. And to keep you safe."

"Evan," she says my name softly but as it rings through the air to me, I hear the threat that comes with it. Her eyes pierce through me as she stares back at me.

"You'll come back to me, every night. Every fucking night. You'll message me back every time I text you."

"I can't text you back from my phone." Her eyes narrow and I'm quick to come up with a solution as I offer, "But I can get another."

"I don't like you doing this," she tells me and I remind her, "I promise it's almost over."

"Evan, you better never do this shit to me again."

"I promise, baby. I promise."

"We can get through anything, but never this again," she whispers and I know I have her. I have her back and I'll be damned if I ever let her feel lonely again.

CHAPTER 24

Kat

Please let me hold you,
I wish he would say.
Please let me hold you,
Please let me stay.

If I can't have him,
My heart has flown.
If I can't have him,
I'd rather be alone.

THE MICROWAVE BEEPS but I have no desire to eat the left-over meatballs from the bistro anymore. I'm shaken to my core. My emotions are all over the place and I'm afraid to believe that we're truly back together.

"Do you want some?" I ask Evan as I shut the microwave door.

He shakes his head and I toss the bowl down carelessly, the ceramic clinking so loud I almost think it broke.

"Talk to me," Evan says again and I want to. God I do, but there's so much to say.

"You want to hear what I've been wanting to tell you for weeks?" I say and even to my own ears I sound like I've lost it.

"Kat, you-"

He's mid-word, a word I don't even give a fuck about. I don't care what he has to say, I'm going to lay it all out there for him and he can choose whatever he wants to do with it. "I'm exasperated. Just because you said sorry doesn't take away everything. I'm still… *feeling*." I can see myself spiraling and I let it happen. "I feel like someone's run over my body with a truck and then backed up. My hips and back hurt. I can't sleep. And that's just the pregnancy." I take a deep breath and continue before he can interrupt me.

"You know, the baby you put in me? That's still happening and by the way, pregnancy doesn't just pause.

So I'm dealing with hormones, and I cry way too much for no reason. I feel sick and I can't sleep. I'm paranoid and I feel so alone that I'm truly scared. I feel crazy and I don't even know what part of this is normal and what part isn't." The words leave me in a fluid mix of emotions. Like a purge of everything I've been feeling, piling up until it drowned me.

Evan doesn't react. If anything I expect him to tell me to calm down. To give me another excuse. I anticipate feeling like I need to change and I'm the one who needs to be fixed. But that's not what happens.

"I want to hold you," is all Evan says. I'm caught, feeling shaky and uncertain as I stand in front of him in nothing but a t-shirt in our kitchen. "I want to make all the pain go away; I'll take it from you," he says and then Evan slips closer to me, wrapping a hand around my waist and I can feel myself falling back into the same trap. 'Cause he does that to me. He makes the pain go away and he makes it so easy to give in.

"Stop," I beg him. "It's like history repeating itself." I swear my body and my thoughts are at war with each other.

"It's not," Evan tells me, his voice begging me and my body persuading me to once again fall into his arms.

"We have a baby coming and I can't put this baby through

the same stupid shit, Evan," I admit to him my fears. "I'm afraid every time I cry the baby can feel it. I think I'm hurting him already." As I say the words, tears prick my eyes.

"Him?" Evan asks. "You think we're having a boy?" The look in his eyes is pure devotion.

"Don't change the subject," I tell him seriously although it warms my heart slightly. "I want you, Evan. But I want you here with me and committed to me and this baby."

"I know," he says and starts to say more but my own fears beg me to confess. "I love you, I love you with everything in me and I won't stop proving that to you every day for the rest of our lives."

"Evan, if you hurt me," I start to threaten him, "I swear I can't take it anymore."

"Never again. I can't stand not being with you," he tells me and my body succumbs to a warmth that's been there all along, just waiting beneath the surface.

He pulls me into his arms and I let him. Even more, I grip onto his shirt as he wraps his muscular arms around me and I breathe in his scent.

My eyes shut tight as he whispers so close to me that my hair tickles my neck as it moves. "I want to make it all better."

He says the right words. He's always been good at that.

He lowers his lips to the shell of my ear. "I only want to love you and have you love me back."

It's been a roller coaster of emotions and my poor heart barely survived. I suppose it's only beating still because it hasn't belonged to me in years. It's always been his.

I nod my head and look down at his chest, inhaling his scent that I've missed for so long and feeling his touch that I've been craving.

"You're still wearing your jacket," I say softly as I run the tips of my fingers down the zipper. I lift my gaze to his dark eyes, swirling with desire. "Take it off," I tell him.

I bite into my lower lip and take half a step back as he keeps his eyes on mine and slips his jacket down his shoulders.

"Your shirt," I breathe and in an instant, he tugs it over his head and carelessly drops it to the floor. He closes the space between us as desire spikes in my blood. Like the first night I saw him, knowing he was trouble, yet I can't resist.

"What now?" Evan asks, moving his pointer finger to the bottom of the cotton t-shirt and letting it slip upward, tugging ever so gently until he reaches the peaks of my breasts. He closes his fingers around my nipples and tugs.

The sensation is directly linked to my clit and it forces me to part my lips with a soft moan. "What now, baby?"

"Mmm," I manage, that's all I can offer as lust clouds my judgment.

"How about this?" Evan suggests and then he unbuckles his belt. The sound of his pants being unzipped fills the small kitchen and my body aches to reach out for him.

His pants fall to the floor and he pushes his boxers down with them, stepping out of them and exposing his thick cock to me.

A rough chuckle distracts me from focusing on his erection and I look into his eyes.

"You still want me?" he asks me and it's only then that my cheeks warm with a blush. My body sways slightly. I murmur my answer, "Mm-hmm."

Evan runs the same pointer from my upper thigh, past my panties and traces the seam along the middle of the cotton, brushing my throbbing clit and sending sparks of heated pleasure through my body.

"I'm the stupid one," he tells me and I only moan in response.

"Tell me," he says as he pushes his fingers under the thin fabric and runs them along my pussy. My body caves forward as he pushes with just the right pressure against my clit and then nearly slips into me as he runs his fingers back down. My fingers fly up to his chest, gripping onto his for balance as my toes curl and my body begs me to ride his fingers.

"Tell me," he says again and then stops. My heavy-lidded eyes open and I pull back to object. "Tell me you still want me."

"I still want you," I say and the words rush out of my lips with need and desperation. Before the last word is even spoken, Evan splays his hand on my lower back and pulls me closer to him, forcing my chest against his.

"Fuck, you're so wet," he groans in the crook of my neck as he forces two fingers deep inside of me. I scream out, clinging to him as the sensation nearly topples me over.

"Evan," I cry out his name, but he doesn't answer as the pleasure builds. It's been so long but I don't remember it ever being like this.

It's so intense, so overwhelming that I know I can't stand for this.

"Evan," I plead for him to understand, but my head flies back and strangled moans fill the air, both from him and from me as I cum on his fingers.

My body buckles and shakes as the orgasm rocks through

me. I'm paralyzed as Evan moves me to the counter. It's cold and hard and I lean against it for balance as slow waves continue to flow through my body.

"And your shirt?" Evan asks me as if I didn't just experience the orgasm of my life.

I grip onto the counter to catch my breath, staring at him.

"I want it off," he says and with my back to his chest, he pulls the shirt off of me. "And these," he tells me, pushing his hand back down my panties. I'm trapped, my back to his front and his strong arm pinning me to him, his other hand on my hip, keeping me still.

My fingers clutch at his wrist and my nails dig in as he strums my sensitive clit.

"Evan," I groan as my body collapses forward and I struggle to take more.

He's not gentle with his strokes in the least. And I love it. My nipples pebble and my body goes weak with a numbing, blinding intensity.

The pleasure stirs deep in my belly but like a flame it grows hotter and hotter, warming me and threatening just the same.

It's only when I cum again that Evan slowly pulls my

panties off of me, leaving them sitting in a puddle by my feet. I'm not blind to the fact that they're soaking wet.

Evan moves his hard erection between my thighs and I widen my stance slightly. He kisses my ear as he runs the head of his dick up and down my pussy. A shiver runs along my body. Every inch is covered with a heated pleasure so sensitive to touch that I go off from just his hot breath on my neck.

"I love you, Kat," Evan whispers as he pushes himself deep inside of me. Slowly, stretching my walls. My head falls back onto his shoulder as he wraps his arm in front of me, pinning me to him. He reaches up and grabs my throat.

Buried deep inside of me, he whispers, "Tell me you love me."

"Always," the word slips out easily, my eyes still closed. I slowly open them to see Evan's expression. I'm struck by the intensity of his gaze. The need, the desire, the possession. "Say the words," he commands.

"I'll always love you," I tell him softly, the words barely audible.

He crashes his lips against mine as he bucks his hips. The sudden spike of near pain makes me push my head back and scratch along his forearm. He doesn't stop, he pounds into me, letting the pleasure build.

He pistons his hips relentlessly, each thrust forcing a pleasured groan from me. I try not to, I try to be quiet, but I can't.

I cum again and again, each climax feeling more intense than the last. Evan's ravenous as he kisses me. He doesn't stop letting his hands roam along my body. He doesn't stop until I have nothing left and only then does he bury himself balls deep into me and cum.

Diary Entry 7

Mom,

I think I've lost my mind.

Evan's like a tornado in my life.

And I think I'm okay with it.

It's bad that I'm worried he's going to leave me again and that I'm scared to believe him, but that I'm okay with trying again, isn't it?

I'm ready to fight for him, Mom.

When he tries it again, I'm not going to let him.

No threats. None of that, I'm simply not going to let him.

I'll be the crazy wife he made me be.

Is that okay? It's probably not. But I don't care.

I love him. I love what he does to me when he's with me. I know I can't be there all the time, but I'm going to have a grip on him.

He promised me and I don't think he's ever broken a promise to me.

I won't let him do something that hurts me again. Although I don't think he will either. That's why I've lost my mind and gone crazy. He just did it not even a month ago, yet I don't think he will again.

Mom, I'm afraid you'd be ashamed of me if you were still here. That's what hurts.

But believe me when I tell you that I love him.

And I believe him when he tells it to me, because I feel it. That hole I was telling you about before? It's the one that came when you left, but it's not there when Evan's with me.

I think he has a hole in his heart too, Mom.

And I think I'm the only one that can fill it.

I told you I've gone crazy, haven't I?

Maybe it's not the worst thing in the world though. I don't know. I don't think I care about it much anymore. So long as I keep Evan close to me.

Even if he doesn't, I'll yank his ass back to where he belongs.

I HOPE I make you proud. And if not, I'm sorry, Mom.

CHAPTER 25

Evan

Clenched fists shake,
With knuckles turning white.
Prepare to let it out,
The beast inside will fight.
Revenge will taste so sweet,
To make right the bitter wrong.
Only time is left,
He can't run for long ...

THE PAPER RUSTLES in my hand. It's a list Pops left on the counter. He didn't tell me about it, but I'm sure it was for us.

Bottles.

Pacifiers.

Bibs.

Onesies.

It goes on for a bit, but it's shit I need to buy I'm sure.

Mason says I need to be seen in public, make sure the tail James has on me sees me keeping my distance, moving on. He wants them to back off and that means I need to look like I'm backing off too.

I look down the aisle as a kid runs past, making swooshing noises and holding a plane up in the air. It's crazy that one day, I'm going to have one of them. A kid. A baby first. And before that, a pregnant wife.

It's fucking terrifying.

"Hey," I call out as the young guy in a blue Kiddie Korner t-shirt walks by with a clipboard in his hand. He has to push his glasses up when he looks at me. "Can I help you, sir?" he asks me.

"Yeah, I was looking for simple baby things. Like bottles and tiny clothes. Things like that," I tell him. "I can't find them anywhere in here."

"We don't have infant merchandise. You'll have to go to

Little Treasures," he says and starts walking to the center of the store to point. "Two blocks down and make a right. It's a bit of a walk, but it's right there on your left."

"Thanks," I reply and slip the paper back into my pocket. If there's a way to get Kat to really forgive me, I know it's to be the best dad I can be. I hope I don't fuck that up too. Although I'm sure I will.

I rub my tired eyes and then walk out of the shop, hearing the ding of the bells above my head and am instantly greeted with the bitter cold.

Just as I'm shoving my hands into my pockets, I see Detective Bradshaw.

"It's one of those days," I mutter beneath my breath as he kicks off the wall. Guess the prick was waiting for me.

"Mr. Thompson," he says as he walks over to me.

I take a few steps forward as a couple of kids run behind me and into the store. Meeting him halfway I answer him, "Detective Bradshaw, nice to see you again." *Not fucking really.*

He huffs a laugh like he heard my thought and says, "I'm glad I found you here."

"A bit odd that we just happened to run into each other," I tell him, holding his gaze and letting him know that I know he must've been following me. "Not my usual hangout."

"Yeah, I noticed. Your schedule's a bit different now?" he says like it's a question.

"A bit."

"For the best, I hope?" he asks.

"Yeah," I say and my word comes out hard. My back's still and my muscles are wound tight. "You taking me in?" I ask him.

I wait as he assesses me, enjoying the suspense.

"Should I?" he asks.

"I can't think of any reason off the top of my head," I tell him.

He doesn't think my answer's funny in the least. My lips quirk up into a smirk at his hardass expression.

"I'm good to go then?" I ask.

"You got any new information for me?" he answers back and gets to the point of this meeting.

"I got nothing to say."

"Why are you doing this to yourself? Protecting someone who wants to issue harassment charges?" he asks me and

I can't help that my forehead creases with both confusion and anger.

"Oh," Detective Bradshaw says, finally showing a little joy. "You didn't hear?" He rocks on his feet, like he's so happy to deliver the news. "James Lapour wanted for us to keep you away from him. He filed for a restraining order and all."

"That's why you're here?" I ask him.

"He said you were snooping around, making him uncomfortable and issuing threats."

"Threats?" I echo, getting angrier and angrier by the second.

"Nothing solid we could work with, so I thought I'd give you a shadow."

"Ah, and thus this wonderful meeting," I answer him, not daring to ask any more or give him anything else. I don't talk to cops. Never have, never will. Half the city's cops are in someone's back pocket.

"I'm sorry to say, I couldn't really give two shits about James Lapour."

Detective Bradshaw's less than pleased with my disinterest. "Just thought you'd like to know."

"Thanks Detective, am I good to go now?"

"Have a good day," he mutters as he walks past me, brushing my shoulder as he goes.

I finally bring my hands out of my pocket and see my clenched fist and the scrap of paper balled up. My breathing comes in shorter and my blood heats.

This shit has to stop. Right fucking now.

DIARY ENTRY 2

DEAR POPS,

I'M ASHAMED. I feel like I've lost complete control and I know it's hurting Kat.

Help me be a better husband and take the nightmares away. Please. Just get them out of my head.

It's just getting worse every night, and it's scaring my wife.

What kind of a man am I? Dreams are tearing my life apart.

I can't sleep without seeing you. Don't get me wrong, I love and miss you so damn much. But you always die in my dreams. You're just gone. All of the memories of our life together are changing. I don't want them to, but I don't know how to stop it.

I have them with Kat too and it's killing me.

I yelled last night and it woke me up. Kat was crying next to me, Pops. She said she'd been trying to wake me up and that's when I started screaming.

She's worried, and I feel like less of a man and husband because I can't stop it.

Please Pops, if you're there and you're able, please help me.

I miss you. I can't stand this.

Please just take it all back.

CHAPTER 26

Kat

Leave me,
Control me,
Make me wait in vain.
You think you own my heart,
You think you can play this game.
I should resist,
I should hate you,
I should leave you in the past.
You gambled with my heart,
But you knew my love would last.

AT WHAT POINT *did this become my life?*

I've been asking myself that question all morning. I've showered, I've eaten and cleaned most of the townhouse. But my mind is fuzzy with disbelief.

I gently shake my head at the thought and then hail a taxi just outside our townhouse. The winter weather has lightened up some, and I almost feel like I could wear a light jacket and not this heavy wool coat. Maybe I've just gotten used to the cold.

If an author submitted my story to me as a manuscript, I'd tell them it's too unbelievable. What's that quote from Mark Twain? Something about how truth is stranger than fiction because fiction needs to make sense.

"Where to, miss?" the cabbie asks me as I sit in the back seat and close the door.

"Saks on Fifth, please," I say confidently although my nerves creep up. Evan would kill me if he knew what I was doing. But it's not going to stop me. I need this.

There are only two things I'm certain of.

I can't afford to let Evan leave me again or else I'll truly lose my mind.

And I'm not going to stay out of this like Evan wants.

The car moves forward, taking me away from the empty townhouse. He's gone off to meet with Mason and tell him what we agreed on. He's staying with me, committing to me and our baby. And he promised to make an effort to move past this. I'll listen to what he tells me to do, but every night he comes back to me. No more secrets and hiding. I have to help him not let the fear of might happen ruin what we have in the present.

I'm still pissed that Mason knew when I didn't. It's a second knife in my back, but I let it slide simply because it's not his ring on my finger.

Instead I focus on the real target here. Samantha Lapour. I'm not over her being with him when we were separated. The hate and jealousy … it's still there.

She loves Fifth Avenue. What rich woman doesn't?

I remember her bragging about her apartment above Saks when I first met her. She was so happy to keep it even though they were happily married.

That should've been my first clue.

The cabbie stops before I'm ready and it's only then that the weight of what I'm doing makes my stomach churn.

"Thank you," I tell the cabbie and pay him, slipping out and onto the curb to avoid the traffic.

My heart beats faster and faster as I make my way through the throngs of people and into the apartment foyer, disappearing from the crowd and readying myself to knock on her door on the fourteenth floor. Her favorite number, as she so joyfully bragged to me once.

I don't know the address though. There are only so many up here, so if at first I don't succeed, I'll simply try again.

My legs are shaky as I climb the stairs; I should have taken the elevator.

"Good evening," a woman's voice says and I have to raise my gaze to watch an older woman with short white hair and a small Pomeranian in her arms close the door to 1401. There are only two other apartments on this floor, the one I'm sure Samantha told me about.

But that was years ago …

"How are you?" I greet the woman as if I'm supposed to be here and slowly open up my purse. I'm sure it looks like I'm getting a key out or maybe my phone to call a friend.

She simply smiles and carries on her way, not even answering the question. I hesitate, looking between the two doors and wondering which one I should knock on first.

This is crazy.

My heart races and a mix of adrenaline and anxiety make me question why I'm even here.

And the real answer, the absolute truth hisses in the back of my head.

She was with him. In his house.

Two confident strides and I knock, one, two, three times on 1402. I don't breathe until I take a small step back and wait.

Silence. No response. The confidence threatens to leave, but the moment I take a step to the right, to knock on the only other option, the door opens.

In red silk pajamas and her hair in curlers, she looks so much different from any other time I've seen her. Samantha wasn't expecting company, that's for sure.

The look on her face is irritation at first and then she recognizes me.

"Oh, hello," she says as she stands up straighter. "Kat."

I have to clear my throat before I can answer her. "Samantha," I greet her in the same stiff way. "I'm sorry to come over with no notice, I was just hoping I could talk to you."

I clutch my purse with both hands. "It's about Evan."

She crosses her arms, instantly looking as though she's on the defensive and I'm quick to add, "I'm worried about him. About the loss of his father and how he's handling it." The words are the truth and the emotion that comes with them is genuine. But I just want an in so I can feel this bitch out.

"I'm so sorry for your loss," she says tightly, still looking me up and down and considering what to do.

"I know you've spent a little time with him and I was just hoping you could tell me how he is."

She nearly flinches and then has to take a moment before she can answer. As if she has no idea how he's doing. Or maybe she's shocked that I know she's seen him, but it's all over the papers, so why wouldn't I know?

Evan's told me one side of this story, but there are always three sides … sometimes even more. And in this case, I'll stay away from James, but I'm sure Samantha will have a thing or two to say.

Although she may not tell me shit.

Either way, now that I know what's going on and that she's played a part in this, I needed to come here. Face to face, without Evan to influence anything. I need this for me.

"Did you guys talk at all?" I ask her. My throat tightens as I add, "He doesn't talk to me at all anymore."

"Oh God," Samantha says and then tells me, "We didn't talk about his father. I'm sorry." She struggles to figure out her words. "I'm sure it's difficult and I understand you two are going through something, but I assure you that I'd like to stay out of it."

She starts to close the door in my face, but I'm quicker.

My palm smacks against the door and I tell her, "I just need someone to talk to. Please! If you could just let me in."

My heart beats as I wait, the door remaining right where it is, only slightly cracked. She opens it slowly, pursing her lips and looking more irked than anything else. As she lets go of the frame, it opens from my weight and she nods her head, letting me in.

"What is it that you want?" she asks as she walks with her back to me inside of the apartment. I close the front door myself and take the place in.

It's a fucking disaster.

I almost ask her if she was robbed, but looking to my left, at a cluttered kitchen I can easily spot three small bags of white powder. And I'm ashamed to say I come to my own conclusions. Right next to them is a colorful bag of pills. A mix of what could be Adderall and pain meds.

She turns with a smirk on her lips. "Like the place?" she asks sarcastically. "My prick of an ex made sure to sell all my shit when I went out of town."

"Oh my God," I say, the words coming out in a whisper of disbelief. There's only a sofa in the living room, a sleek gray contemporary sectional. I imagine it would look beautiful if the living room itself wasn't vacant of any other piece of furniture. She settles down onto one end and I take the other.

Glancing up at the chandelier I tell her, "I'm so sorry. I'm sure it was beautiful … " my voice trails off and she doesn't say anything.

"You could go to the cops," I offer her and she laughs with ridicule.

"He's got them all, sweetheart. I'm barely surviving."

"I am so sorry," I say, at a loss for words and feeling so much more uncomfortable than I anticipated. I even feel bad for her to some degree.

"Divorce isn't always a bad thing, love," she says and then takes in my expression. "I'm sorry for you two though, I really am."

It's hard to judge her tone, so I'm not sure how to take it.

"I actually had something to ask you about your husband," I say as Samantha reaches for a pack of cigarettes and takes one out.

She lights it and then asks, "What's that?"

There's a glint in her eyes and her back stiffens slightly.

"Evan doesn't like him much," I tell her, gauging her reaction and she lets out a small laugh that's accompanied with smoke.

"I don't much like the asshole either."

"Can't blame you," I say as I set my purse down beside me and feign a casualness I don't feel.

"He told me he thinks James is trying to kill him." I hold her gaze as I say, "I think he's paranoid."

Samantha takes a long pull of her cigarette, ignoring the question until I tell her.

"I was hoping that if I talked to you, you could tell me the truth. Evan's just being crazy, isn't he?" I say with my heart racing.

Every nerve is on edge in my body. There's something about how she looks at me. As if she's wondering what to do with me.

I don't trust it, and I don't trust her.

"Evan told you what now?" she asks.

"Evan told me that James tried to kill him, thinking he'd do coke left out for him."

"Did he?" she says so condescendingly. "I'm surprised, because from what he told me, he didn't want you to know."

I hate her in this moment. I hate the straight expression of disinterest.

I hate that Evan was with her when he should have been with me.

I hate that she knew he was keeping secrets.

"It was a mistake on his part," I tell her, my fingers tensing as I grip onto my purse harder. Her expression changes slightly, but only slightly with a raised brow and the hint of a smirk. Amusement. I fucking hate her.

"Maybe it was a mistake to come here. I thought you'd know or maybe get a sense of how Evan's doing since you were with him."

"I have no idea what you're talking about," she tells me as she puts out the cigarette into a mug that's sitting on her furnace.

"My apologies then," I say, shrugging it off. I stand up, readying myself to leave, but I can't keep my mouth shut. I can't not say something to this lying bitch.

"One quick question … did you enjoy fucking my husband?" I ask her and she lets out a condescending laugh.

"He tells you lots of things, doesn't he?" she says with a smirk on her face.

"He used to. It's more for curiosity's sake," I say, turning slightly toward the door so she can see I'm on my way out.

"It was years ago and I can assure you it must not have been memorable."

"Well I suppose that's a win for me then," I say with a smile and make my way to her front door, looking over my shoulder once again at the poor state of this woman's home.

"I wish you well," I tell her as I leave, opening and closing the door myself. And I'm more than happy to never see that bitch again.

If Evan thinks for one minute he's going to see her again, for any reason, he's fucking wrong.

CHAPTER 27

Evan

Kisses tell a tale,
The touch so raw and sweet.
Eyes closed and heart open,
When our lips will meet.
I'm meant to feel your desire,
And fall victim to your taste.
Kisses tell a tale indeed,
There is no time to waste.

"What'd you do today?" Kat asks me as I turn the stove on, listening to the clicks before the gas lights.

"Not much," I answer her as I look over my shoulder. *Just*

hunting down the identity of a drug dealer. I grind my teeth at the thought, wishing it weren't true.

"What do you think you want to do?" Kat asks me as I pour olive oil into the pan. Chicken marsala for dinner. My throat goes dry as I remember how Pops taught me how to cook it; it was one of his favorites.

"Like do for work?" I ask her and put the chicken in the pan. The sizzle is perfect.

She shrugs and then hops up on the counter, setting her ass down and letting her feet dangle. "I know you have some investments."

"Some is putting it lightly," I tell her. "If you're worried about money, don't be. We'll be fine." I haven't checked in a week or two on some of the stocks, but the savings account is more than enough. We've been here so long, both of us working and not doing much of anything else. The money just piled up.

"I'm not really worried about money, it's more about what you're going to do with yourself."

I flip the breasts over and pick up the pan, making sure to spread the oil before setting it back down. Just how Ma used to do.

"We have the baby," I tell her and walk over, standing

between her legs with my hands at her hips. "That's all I've been thinking about for now."

"The baby won't be here for a while," she tells me and threads her fingers through my hair. I love it when she does this. When she loves on me. I missed this. "I'm worried about you," she tells me and I back away slightly, but she keeps me there, tightening her legs around me.

"Don't be upset," she says and I find it hard not to be.

"I'm fine," I tell her and even I know it's a lie.

"You just lost your father, and … "

"Stop worrying about me," I tell her.

"You scared me last night with the night terror. And the ones you've had before," she adds. I shouldn't have told her.

"It'll be over soon," I reassure her and get back to cooking. It's quiet for a moment, but that doesn't last long. Kat's not the best at giving up on what she wants.

"But what do you *want* to do?" she asks me. At least she dropped the subject about Pops and the nightmares.

I look back at her, wiping my hands with the kitchen towel and then tossing it on to the countertop.

"I'm not worried about keeping myself busy," I tell her.

She purses her lips and nods, but she doesn't seem convinced.

"I'm going to be fine," I say and stir the sauce before layering it onto the cooked chicken.

"You know what I'm going to do?" I ask her and ignore the pit in my stomach about everything going on. I just focus on after all this shit is over.

"I'm going to move us out of here," I say and she rolls her eyes.

"For the love of God, hire a moving company this time," she says with exasperation and I give her the laugh she's after.

"I'm going to find a house you love and help you make it ours." I tap the tongs on the side of the pan as I pull it off the burner and then walk back to her. "I'm going to set up our baby's room and make it perfect."

She likes that. She starts swaying on the counter like she's giddy at the thought.

"I'm going to make sure the two of you have nothing to worry about and that the three of us are happy and healthy and all that good shit."

She lets out a small laugh and wraps her arms around my shoulders.

"I love you, babe," I tell her and she leans in for a small kiss.

"I love you too, and I just hate seeing you anything other than happy."

"I'll be better when this is over with," I tell her. She kisses me soft and sweet, and it feels right. She's a balm to my soul, but it doesn't take the pain away.

"I'm worried for you," she whispers against my lips.

I brush my nose against hers. "It's not supposed to work that way," I tell her.

Her green eyes peek up at me through her thick lashes and she says, "Yeah it is. Don't you know that by now?"

CHAPTER 28

Kat

I want us back,
The way we used to be.
Accept what's done is done,
And move on with me.
Just hold my hand and walk in strides,
The path is clear to see.
Just hold my hand, it's yours to take,
You were meant to be with me.

"I THOUGHT we were just going to order out," Evan says from across the table. The silverware clinks in his hand as he picks up the white cloth napkin and lays it over his lap.

The Savinga Grill has always been one of my favorite restaurants since I first discovered it years ago. Exposed dark red brick, raw wood beams and high ceilings. It's rustic, it's cozy, and it's only a cab away.

That's what I told Evan to get him here when he asked where I wanted to go. *Just a cab away.*

I shrug and say, "I just wanted to go out."

"It makes me nervous," he says.

I lay my hand on the table, palm up and wait for him to take it. "Mason said you need to be seen."

"Me, not *us*." He emphasizes the word us.

"It's part of us moving forward together." The smile on my lips is small but it's still there. "I won't let someone keep me from you or us from our lives."

His lips twitch with a response, but instead he doesn't say anything.

"We tried this your way, now we try it mine," I tell him and my words come out hard.

"And your way is to go out in public?" he asks me.

"I want us out, yes." My answer is blunt as I pull my own napkin across my lap. "I'm not going to hide away in some hotel and let my fear cripple me." My voice is stern but also sympathetic. "If someone wants to know if we're together, let them know." He woke up last night with sweat pouring down his face. He was screaming in his sleep. I refuse to play this psychological game. I'm going to be there for my husband. I'm going to do everything I can to make him better. And that means not hiding and not being scared. I'll be strong for him.

"I won't let a single person keep us from moving on with our lives. And that means being together and going to my favorite restaurant to celebrate."

I flash him a smile as the waiter walks over to us. Like this conversation doesn't put me on edge.

It's quiet while the water is being poured and stays that way with the exception of the waiter telling us the specials and handing us the menus.

It's only when he leaves us that I continue what I was saying.

"Yes, I want us to be seen. I also want to celebrate being pregnant. I want to buy a new house, a bigger one closer to the park." I pick up the water, resting my elbow on the table as I talk while reading the menu, even though I already know what I want. "I want to slow down with work and I want the world to know it all. And if they don't care, don't like it or want to stop us," I lean forward and whisper, "then fuck them."

He only responds with a tight smile.

"I'm not going to let this change us and who we are."

"I don't want you to be in danger," he answers me.

"Too late, baby," I say and my smile falters.

"I feel really uncomfortable being here," he tells me and it upsets me. He needs to move on.

"And I feel like you're perpetuating your fears by hiding away and only focusing on them. Not just focusing, but allowing them to dictate everything," I tell him and my voice cracks. I have to take a sip of water to calm myself down. "I hate what you allowed to happen simply because you were afraid of an outcome that may or may not ever be a possibility."

"You don't understand," he tells me with a frustrated sigh and it pisses me off.

"It felt like you'd died," I admit to him. "So I think I do." I take another drink of water and then ask, "What if the cops stop looking? What if James gets away with it? What then?"

He doesn't answer, although I can see his will to fight me has left.

"I just want us back," I admit to him. "That's really what it comes down to."

This time it's him who puts his hand on the table and I'm more than happy to reach for him.

He kisses my knuckles and then my wrist. "I'm sorry," he says again. He keeps telling me that he's sorry.

"I know you are, but what am I?" I give him a joking response to lighten the mood and it works somewhat.

As Evan's lips pull into a smile and he relaxes his posture, he takes my hand in his.

"You know I miss this side of you?" he tells me.

"What side?"

"The playful side," he says and squeezes my hand … kind of like how my heart squeezes.

"Can I tell you a secret?" I ask him as the waiter walks up to us. "I miss it too."

"Are you two ready to order?" the waiter asks, looking between both of us and clasping his hands in front of him.

"You first," Evan says and gestures at me.

"The lasagna please, with a house salad." I almost order a

glass of cabernet but then I stop myself. Every time I remember we're having a baby it's a gift in itself.

"And I'll have the same," Evan says and it surprises me.

"You never have lasagna."

He shrugs and says, "I guess I just wanted to try it your way."

"We have the doctor's appointment coming up and since you're no longer working, I assume you're coming with?" I ask him as the waiter leaves us.

"Of course," Evan says and then he leans forward. "You know you look beautiful, right?"

He's so cheesy but I can't help the smile and blush. "Stop," I brush him off.

"Never," he says playfully.

That warm cheery feeling in my chest slowly drifts away as I remember my own little secret. Not so little really.

"I have something to tell you," I spit the words out at the risk of upsetting Evan. "I did something that I don't think you're going to like."

"What's that?" he asks easily although I notice his shoulders stiffen.

"I was curious about something and I think it's something only I would know how to ask appropriately ... "

I don't know how to word this and I find myself staring at the ice in the glass of water.

"You can tell me," Evan says as if it's no big deal. "Whatever it is."

"I went to see Samantha yesterday. At her place on Fifth Avenue," I tell him, confessing before I can stop myself. The air instantly changes as Evan doesn't respond. He seems uncomfortable, if anything.

"I had to know for myself."

"What did you have to know?" he asks me, shifting in his seat. He leans forward like he's going to scold me and I can already hear it. Danger this and that. Harm's way, etcetera, etcetera.

"I had to know if she was your type. What she was like. So I know how to react when her name comes up."

Evan runs his hand down the back of his head as he looks away from me. As if it's stupid of me. "You don't understand-" I start to explain but he cuts me off.

"There's no one else for me, Kat," he tells me bluntly, his hands hitting the table and rattling the small plates. The couple a table down from us glances in our direction and Evan calms down.

"I knew you would be upset-" I start to say and again he cuts me off.

"But you did it anyway."

I nod my head once. "I did. And it's over."

The tension between us thins a bit as I look him in the eyes and say, "It's over. There's nothing there and I'm fine now."

"You're fine?" he asks me.

"Yeah," I tell him and I am. "There's no way she's your type."

My response gets a short laugh from Evan. A genuine smile even. "You know you're crazy?" he asks me.

"I do. And you made me this way."

"Fair enough," he says but then his expression gets serious.

"I know, don't do it again," I say before he can tell me.

"I'm serious," he says and I nod.

I look toward the front of the restaurant, to the right of

Evan as another couple walks in. "I was surprised that Samantha does drugs." I say absently. More to gossip than anything else. Well, maybe to throw her under the bus a little. I can admit that I'm not a big enough woman not to.

"What?" Evan asks.

"There was coke on her kitchen table." He looks back at me with an expression that's not quite disbelief, but something else.

"Coke?" he asks me. "Sam doesn't do drugs."

I ignore the fact that he called her Sam and nod my head once while I add, "And a bag of pills. She had a variety pack, Adderall and a mix of things. It was like a grab bag. I never would have guessed she does drugs," I tell him and wait for him to say something.

"Speed?" he asks me again although it's not quite spoken like a question.

"I didn't say speed," I tell him.

"Adderall is speed," he tells me with a concerned expression.

"Oh I didn't know. And I'm just guessing it's Adderall." I'm not exactly the best at drug identification. I swallow thickly, wishing I'd just kept my mouth shut and saved the gossip for the girls.

I watch as his forehead pinches. But there's something else in his expression that catches me off guard. It's hard and unforgiving. Even his hands clench into fists on top of the table. I glance at them and then his eyes, but movement behind him at the front of the restaurant catches my attention.

"Is that Suzette?" I ask Evan as I think I spot her walk in. I don't think I've ever been happier for a change in conversation. It's definitely her. I'd know that bob anywhere. She walks slowly as she digs in her purse, looking for something at the front of the restaurant.

I'm pushing my chair out from the table when my mouth drops open at the sight of a man coming up from behind her.

He's much taller than her and in her heels, Sue is already taller than me. I don't recognize him; he's facing away from me. But in a black suit he stalks up behind her, letting his hand stray to her waist and pulling her close to him.

"Who is that?" I say beneath my breath but when I look to Evan and try to get his attention, he's busy on his phone.

"Babe," I not so quietly try to get his attention. It's not every day you see one of your good friends being felt up by someone you don't know.

I have to turn my head when I look back up to keep my eyes on them and try to follow them down the hall. But they're gone before I even get the chance to stand.

I swear it was her and I go to reach for my phone, but glancing at Evan stops me mid-reach.

"What's wrong?" I ask him as he stares at his phone.

"We have to go," he says.

"We just got here," I object, but that doesn't stop him from standing up abruptly as the waiter returns to our table.

"I'm so sorry, we have to go," Evan tells the waiter. "Please cancel the order."

"Are you serious?" I ask him as the couple from before looks at us again.

"I'm sorry, but something just came up," he tells me and there's a look in his eyes that's begging me not to push him. "Please, Kat," he says to me. "Please, we need to leave."

CHAPTER 29

Evan

It was a foolish thing,
To leave your side,
And risk you forgetting who we are.
When we're together,
Everything shifts,
On my heart, you've left a scar.
It's wounded,
And hurts so deep,
But is beautiful nonetheless.
I'm a better man for loving you,
It's a truth that I confess.

"This alley smells like piss," Mason says as we stop in between a Chinese restaurant and a shoe store. I met up with him on Prince Street and we walked our way here. Just me and him … and business to take care of.

I take a whiff and immediately regret it. "This is where he's going though, right?" I ask him.

"Should already be there," he says and nods.

"That's what it said on Instagram. 'Getting ready for the party,'" he says beneath his breath and shoves his hands in his pockets.

It's bitter cold and the city streets are packed with people shopping and moving about like normal.

"I don't believe in coincidences," I tell Mason and bring it up again.

His eyes flicker to me and then back to across the street.

"There's no way she happens to do speed," I tell him. I've known Samantha for a long damn time. "Her husband dabbles in all sorts of drugs recreationally. But she doesn't touch it."

"It's possible she does it on the down low?" he suggests. "You'd be surprised how many people do coke nowadays."

I shake my head. "There has to be a connection between her and the dealer."

"We're gonna find out, aren't we?" he asks me although it's a rhetorical question.

"What's the plan?"

"All we need is an address."

"Just follow him?" I ask with disbelief.

"Only for a bit, then we switch off so we aren't seen."

"Switch off to who?"

"I got some guys," Mason says and frustration gets the best of me.

"I want to be the one-" I start to tell him but he cuts me off.

"You want to keep her safe? Getting into this shit isn't what you need. That's not what the man who deserves to be at Kat's side would do."

That shuts me up, but I fucking hate it.

"So we just wait?" I ask him again.

"Yeah," he says and his breath turns to fog, "just wait."

Almost an hour passes before I think about going back to

Kat. I pull my phone out and debate on messaging her, but James is still watching and I don't have a burner yet.

"Fuck me," I say out loud and run my hands down my face.

"Sorry, you're not my type," Mason says so matter-of-factly from his spot next to me. I grunt a short laugh despite myself. "I feel so fucking trapped."

"I know the feeling," Mason tells me and I give him a side-eye. His stare only hardens. "I know what it's like to be in a lose-lose situation where the stakes are high." He looks forward, staring at the opposite brick wall in the thin alley. "Too high," he mutters beneath his breath.

"So what do you do?" I ask him and get his attention again. "How do you win?" I ask him with all sincerity, as if he has an answer that will put an end to this hell.

He shakes his head as he looks down at the ground and replies, "Sometimes there's not a way to win, just a way to survive."

I have to tear my eyes away from him, knowing he's right and when I do, my arm reaches out and smacks him in the chest.

"Visual," I tell him and Mason doesn't hesitate to take out his phone and call the tail. "He's here," he speaks into the phone as both of us watch the perp, talking to someone in an open doorway on 20th and Broadway. Even from his profile, I know it's him.

Every muscle in my body coils, ready to fight. It's been weeks of holding back and not being able to do anything. And just across the street is the last piece to this puzzle of fucking misery.

Dark black hair, slicked back and tanned skin with a tattoo scrolling up his neck. It's definitely him. We got this prick.

The second he's walking down the stone steps, we're out of the alley and following from across the street. I keep my eyes on him, walking through the thick crowd with my jaw clenched.

"Johnny we got him," Mason talks into his cell phone as we walk. I try not to make it obvious that we're following the fucker. At the same time, I'm holding back every desire to chase the dealer down and beat the shit out of him to get every last bit of information from him.

"Heading down Twenty-Second," I hear Mason say and instinctively I glance up and look at the street sign before turning left to follow the asshole.

My blood's pumping hard and every step it gets harder and harder not to pick up speed.

Right as we get to the end of the block and the crosswalk

sign turns to a red hand, the fucker walks out, ignoring the oncoming cars and nearly getting hit, but he keeps going, yelling at the drivers as if it's their fault. I move to do the same. We can't risk losing him, but Mason puts his arm out in front of my chest to stop me.

"He's got him," he tells me, his eyes on the back of the dealer as he vanishes into the thick crowd. "Johnny's on him."

My shoulders rise and fall with my heavy breaths. I'm calm on the outside, but inside I'm pacing. "I need to do something," I tell him, ignoring how the woman to my right turns back to look at me as if I've lost it. Maybe I have.

"Then go home," Mason tells me and turns halfway around to walk right back up the way we came.

His leather jacket bunches in my fist as I pull him back to me. "I can't sit around and do nothing," I tell him, pleading with him to understand.

"The best thing for you to do is go home to your pregnant wife and stay right the fuck there," Mason tells me.

I swallow thickly, feeling guilt settle in my stomach. "She needs you to be there," he says and I wonder if he's just saying that to make me listen to his order, or if he really means it.

I nod my head reluctantly as the crosswalk sign flips back, and the crowd around us crosses the street.

I hesitate, only for a moment, but then I turn my back and follow Mason to the car. That's when I decide to do what I've been wanting to do for a long damn time. I take out my cell phone and text Kat, *I'm coming home*.

CHAPTER 30

Kat

You can't hide from me,
No matter how hard you try.
I know your tells, I know your thoughts,
Now look me in the eye.
Don't stow away, don't shut me out,
I'm only here for you.
I want to help, I'll ease your pain,
Just tell me what to do.

HE'S ACTING WEIRD.

Ever since we left dinner last night, Evan's been shut off.

He didn't tell me why we had to leave and I'm honestly sick of it. I grit my teeth and gave in to leaving yesterday. I gave him a full day to explain. But I've had enough.

Evan checks his phone again as an explosion on the television booms through the living room. He doesn't flinch or react. He's numb.

I scroll through the list I've added to the baby registry. Maddie sent me a check-off chart and it's so, so long. I was enjoying it though. All the clothes in miniature and every odd and end, from pacifier holders to little mittens.

But even as a small smile slips across my lips and my hand moves to my belly, I'm distracted. Something's wrong with Evan.

I peek up at him again, moving my ass into the cushion and pulling the throw closer to me. "Why do you keep checking your phone?"

"It's nothing," he answers.

I'm slow and deliberate as I push myself into a seated cross-legged position across from my husband on the sofa.

The expression on his face is one I've seen before, the *what is she doing* look.

He sets his phone down beside him, and I don't take my eyes off his, but I notice how he tries to hide it.

"No secrets," I tell him. "You promised."

Another loud boom from the television distracts me and I reach for the remote without hesitation, bending over Evan and grabbing it as it sits right next to his phone. As soon as the television screen goes black, I toss the remote behind me and into the seat where I was just lying.

Giving him my full attention I tell him, "I feel like maybe you have something to tell me." I hold his gaze and his expression gives me nothing.

I'm so close to snatching his phone from him just to prove him wrong, but before I pull the trigger on that idea he says, "I don't want to bother you with these things."

"You're my husband. You're supposed to bother me." I say it with a little humor, but again, he doesn't react.

"Tell me, Evan. I *want* to know." I scoot closer to him, just a bit so my leg touches his and I rest a hand on his thigh.

"It's something you said. About Samantha having drugs." He looks away from me at the far wall in the room. "It's something bad," he adds.

"What about it?" I hate that an inkling of jealousy creeps

up on me, but it's quickly followed by a darker realization.

"The coke that killed Tony was laced with poison. High amounts." He looks me in the eyes and slowly the pieces come together, one by one.

A chill flows over my skin. "Did you tell Mason?" I ask him.

He nods and then confesses, "He thinks he has something concrete."

"What?" I ask him, eager for more. I can't lie that there's a part of me that's afraid though.

"He can't tell me over the phone," Evan says as if that's the end of the discussion.

"Is it good or bad?" I ask him.

"Good I think." Evan nods his head and almost looks teary-eyed. "He said it's done and to come see him."

"It's done?" I ask him, and my lungs stay perfectly still until Evan nods his head once. I cave into him, holding on to him and not wanting to admit how much fear I held deep inside. "It's really over?" I ask him and he shrugs although he looks emotional.

"I have to talk to him." He turns his attention back to the television and then glances at the remote.

It takes me a moment to realize that he's planning on leaving me out of it.

No. Fucking. Way.

"So when are you meeting him?" I ask him, narrowing my eyes as I do.

"When you get in bed," he tells me pointedly and I shake my head and then get up off the couch.

"I'm coming with you," I tell him. My boots are at the front door and I already have socks on.

I don't pay attention to him as he stalks over to the door without bothering to grab his coat off the hook.

"What are you doing?" he asks me as I shove one boot on and then the other.

"I told you," I tell him and then stand upright, grabbing my coat. "I'm coming with you."

I stand there, praying he doesn't shut me out. I need to know.

All of this destroyed me in a way I'll never forget. It broke me and left me in pieces for him to pick up and put back together. He better not deny me this.

"You know I love you, right?" he asks as he steps forward and brushes the hair out of my face.

My eyes flicker from his chest to his eyes as I say, "I do."

His lips twitch into a smile and he leans down to kiss me. It's chaste and quick, but he rests his forehead against mine, his hand still on my jaw.

"I don't like this," he whispers.

I can't respond. The words are caught in my throat and I have nothing to give him.

When he pulls back and looks me in the eyes, he looks like he may object, but he's a smart man and instead he reaches for his coat without a word and opens the door for us to go.

CHAPTER 31

Evan

I was so sure,
I thought I knew—
I thought I knew it all.
But one slight change,
And the truth revealed—
I would have let him take the fall.

Hate and pain,
Turned to poison—
Poison in my blood.
But one slight change,
And the truth revealed—
My revenge drowns in the flood.

"I CAN'T BELIEVE IT." My words come out heavy as I stare down at the paper and then look back to Mason. But I've known since Kat told me. Samantha's the reason that coke was laced and it wasn't meant for me at all. It was James she wanted dead.

Anger rolls through me like a low tide. Slowly rising and each wave threatening to take more and more.

"She was fucking him," Mason says.

"Fucking who?" Kat asks, still clinging to my side. She insisted on coming and at first I didn't want her here. I don't want her involved in this more than I'd already had.

Now though, knowing she went to Samantha, that she spoke to her, and was inside her apartment, so close to a woman capable of murder, I need her here.

The anger dies immediately. It's only gratitude and the still-sharp fear of losing Kat that takes over.

I wrap my arm around her as I look over Mason's shoulder and outside of the picture window in his sitting room. I need to feel her. I need to know she's still here, alive and by my side. Away from any danger.

"Samantha was fucking Andrew, the dealer. They planned to kill James and it went wrong."

"Do you have evidence?" Kat asks and I look down at her. She's standing there as if she just asked for a receipt for an item she wants to return to Nordstrom, not at all affected in the least.

"Plenty of it," Mason answers and I look back at him when I can feel his eyes on me. "Shots of her with Andrew. Pictures of the coke and a sample."

"Are you alright?" I ask Kat and she cranes her neck to look me in the eyes.

"Of course," she answers easily. Her forehead pinches as she asks, "Why?"

"It's just a lot to handle, a lot to deal with," I tell her, once again questioning myself. I let Samantha manipulate me. I didn't even think twice about Kat's safety in Samantha's apartment, not that I would have let her go if I had known.

"She could have killed you," I whisper.

"She could have tried," Kat says back, and then holds me tighter. "But I'm here. And now we've got her."

I nod my head, feeling slight relief, but knowing it's not over until she's behind bars.

"Why would she want James dead?" Kat asks Mason and he's quick to respond.

"The divorce would have given her nothing," he says and I nod my head. Samantha told me that.

"She's the one who cheated and according to their prenup we found in James' office, a divorce would leave her without a damn penny to her name."

"Better to kill him than to get divorced," Kat says under her breath and walks away from me, walking to the far side of the room to pick up the cup of hot tea she left on the side table.

"What about James?" I ask him. "He really had nothing to do with this?"

Mason shrugs. "Still a prick, and now he's onto his wife, but I don't have shit on him."

I break eye contact and wipe a hand down my face. Fuck! I feel like a fool. Guilt and regret swirl together and the mix of emotions makes me numb. I have to remind myself that all I need right now is Kat, just my wife. I'll cling to her until the dust settles.

"You were wrong," Kat says from across the room.

"I would've killed him," I admit to them, and it hurts to do it. The past few nights I've lied awake, thinking about all the ways I considered to murder him. As I stood outside of his house, I knew it'd be easy. I craved to see his body dead on the floor.

"It's because of her, she's the one that fed you lies and made sure you were blaming him," Kat speaks lowly, but her breathing picks up as anger gets the best of her.

"It's not hard to focus on revenge," Mason says as if reading my mind. "It's not your fault for wanting this over so you could protect your wife."

The clink of ceramic on glass gets my attention as Kat sets down her mug and walks back over to me.

"So what do we do now?" Kat asks and then leans her back against my front.

Mason smirks at her and then looks between the two of us. "See, this I love," he says, tapping the folder in his hands.

"Now we leak it. I don't want to kill a woman," Mason says.

"Leak it?" I ask.

"You do the same shit to them that's been done to us," Kat speaks up. "I want it all over every social media platform they have."

"What are you talking about?" Mason asks.

"You can get onto James' computer, right?" Kat asks Mason.

"Yeah."

"He's going to post about how she's fucking a drug dealer. He's going to write all about how he found coke and a grab bag of pills in her office and that's why they've split."

"Drag her through the fucking mud," Kat says and emphasizes every word.

"The cops need to know," I remind her.

"They're itching for something. And this city talks," Mason answers me, nodding his head at Kat's suggestion. "I was thinking of leaking to a man on the inside, but Kat's idea would be easier, less risky."

"You have to drop the dealer's name, both his street and real name." Kat crosses her arms as she looks Mason dead in the eyes and adds, "Make sure you tag her ass in the tweets."

I wish I could joke back to her about being bitter. I wish I felt a sense of relief that this feels like it's finally coming to an end. But I can't and I don't.

"You're a pretty vindictive woman, you know that?" Mason says, obviously amused.

"I just don't like it when a bitch almost kills someone I love. I really don't like her talking in his ear either," she adds and then shrugs. "I can be a little jealous."

I can't force a smile to my lips, although I do love it. I love how possessive she is of me and how she's showing it every chance she can get.

"Is Kat safe?" I ask Mason. "If we intervene and do this, are they going to know?"

"They won't know shit. James will be relieved more than anything else. He's a time bomb of paranoia waiting to go off." Mason backs up, leaning against the back of a sitting chair as he adds, "And Samantha will be behind bars by morning."

"She can't deny the pictures of the evidence."

"She'll make bail."

"With the cops James has in his back pocket?" Mason looks at me with disbelief. "No way. She's done."

"Good," Kat says with finality.

"What really gets me is that she came to me when she didn't have to. Why?"

"To make sure you didn't know it was her," Kat answers me. "You're the only other person involved who was still alive to give up any information at all." My fingers tap along my bottom lip as I remember every meeting I had with her, how she made it so clear to me that James was the one to go after.

"With you focused on James and him on you, she could get away with it."

"That's a thing, you know? The perps go to the cops as witnesses." Mason adds, "That's how they catch them sometimes."

I'm still partially dumbfounded, but I know everything they're saying is true. It all adds up and there's no other explanation. But the need to do something, to fix this myself, is killing me.

"Do you need me to do anything?" I ask Mason as Kat cradles her body into mine.

"I can take it from here, but I'd stay inside and keep a low profile until there's word about the arrest."

I give him a tight smile and then peck Kat's hair. "Let's go home, baby."

One week later

Just one more,
And only one.
This is it,
Till my life is done.
I need this for me,
To be complete.

Just one more,
One last deceit.

"Is he in there?" I ask Mason as we sit in the car.

Andrew Jones, also known as Mathew Staller. The man who sold Samantha the drugs, planned the murder, and got off with nothing. And according to Mason, this isn't the first time that's happened.

He didn't get a single charge that stuck to him. Not a damn thing. Samantha protected him and plead guilty when it came down on her. But Andrew? He got off. Too bad for him.

"Yeah, this is it," Mason answers me as he unbuckles his seatbelt. The click is loud in the still night air.

I watch the light at the end of the street turn green, but there's not a single car down the road where Andrew's house is. Not a person in sight, in fact.

Which is good fucking news. I guess he liked being out here for his privacy, away from the city in a Podunk area … maybe it's where he makes the drugs. Or maybe he's laying low since it all went down only days ago.

I don't know and I don't give a fuck.

As I step out of the car, the chill of the night creeping into my bones, I tell Mason, "You better never tell Kat."

He grins at me and says, "It's our secret."

We close the car doors softly and I keep my eyes on the warm yellow light coming from the upstairs of the two-story house.

"Sticking to the plan?" Mason asks me.

My head nods but I don't take my eyes off the light upstairs. "Let's scope the place out, make sure it's just him." I finally look at Mason and say, "We've got the duct tape and rope in the trunk, right?" It's lined in plastic and ready for Andrew.

"Yeah, the only part that's going to be hard is getting this fucker down so we can tie him up."

I crack my knuckles one by one, all the pent-up anger and fear from the past couple of weeks raging in my blood, begging for revenge.

I would've died. I came so close to dying and losing everything because of this fucker. My wife would have been a pregnant widow. And it's 'cause of this asshole.

"That's not going to be a problem," I tell Mason.

He grins at me. "I'll get the front, you get the back."

But as he tells me, guess who comes right out the front door, hoodie on and walks right out onto the sidewalk.

"I don't do meets here, get the fuck out," he tells us as he walks up to us, only feet from the car.

"Not here?" Mason asks as if we're here to buy or sell or whatever the hell Andrew thinks we're here for.

"Yeah, like I said, I don't do meetings here," Andrew repeats and then opens his coat, flashing a gun tucked in his waistband. "So get the fuck out."

Dumb fuck should have had the gun in his hand.

The rage makes me see red.

I go for the first punch, getting him right in the jaw, my blood rushing in my ear as he and Mason both fumble for the gun. Mason grabs it from him as a bullet goes off, flying through the air and ricocheting off the car. I get in another punch, stunning the dealer. Over and over I slam my fists into him. My teeth grind against one another as I don't hold back a damn thing.

Andrew only gets that one shot off and then the gun clatters to the sidewalk.

Smash! I hear the prick's jaw snap and feel the bones crunch under the weight of my fist. I see the images that haunted me for weeks.

Andrew pulls back his arm and gets me good. But only once and it barely affects me. My head snaps to the side as the punch lands on my chin. I throw all my weight forward, pushing him to the ground and feeling my body fall on top of his, slamming hard onto the concrete sidewalk.

"Fuck!" he screams out just as I pin him under me and land punch after punch. His nose cracks under one of them; I don't know how many I get in. I can't stop. All the fear leaves me as rage.

"Evan!" Mason screams out, pulling me backward, but I get one more hit in that snaps Andrew's head to the side and for a moment, I think he's dead. He lays nearly lifeless. Blood's covering his face and soaking into my knuckles. It's fucking everywhere.

Andrew spits blood onto the street next to him and coughs it up as I try to breathe.

"Snap out of it. It's not in the plan!" Mason screams next to me, or maybe it's not a scream. There's a ringing in my head that won't quit. One that balances out my heavy breathing and the stinging pain that shoots from the split knuckles on my hand.

When I finally catch my breath, I see Mason on top of him on the ground, pinning him down. He knees Mason in the stomach, desperately trying to win a losing fight.

But I'm too quick, grabbing his own gun and shooting him once in his thigh.

I don't want to kill him. That's not my job to do.

He's not for me. But I'll be damned if I didn't love beating the piss out of him.

Andrew screams out in agony and Mason, still wincing and holding his gut, socks him right in the mouth.

"Shut the fuck up," he yells at him. Mason catches his breath as he slowly stands up and Andrew stares up at us, begging for mercy.

"Are you Andrew Jones?" I ask him and he hesitates to answer, so I fire a shot off right next to him.

"Yes!" he screams. "Fuck! Yes!"

I crouch down in front of him, gun still in my hand. "The same Andrew Jones that left those messages for Samantha? The ones convincing her to murder her husband?" The blood drains from his face as I talk. "The same Andrew Jones that gave her poisoned coke so she could end his life and pay you half of what the insurance company was going to give her?"

"I don't … " he tries to lie and I shoot off my gun again, feeling the shockwaves of the trigger run up my arm. It's closer to him this time and Andrew screams out.

“He pissed himself,” Mason says and when I look, sure enough, his sweats have a dark wet ring around him. He’s pathetic.

“That Andrew Jones?” I ask him.

“She wanted him dead!” he yells. “She was going to do it whether I helped her or not.”

“Is that what you think about all the people you’ve helped commit murder?” I ask him. He doesn’t answer and I nod at Mason to grab the shit from the trunk.

“You can tell her husband that; I’m sure he’ll understand,” Mason says and then tosses handcuffs at his feet. “Put those on. First your feet, and then your hands.”

“Please,” he begs. But there’s no mercy for what he’s done.

It takes a good fifteen minutes to tie him up. The gagging was the hardest part.

The trunk slams shut and the dark night seems so empty. Empty is what I needed though. It’s done and over.

Mason turns the car on and we leave in silence, listening to the fucker in the back.

My heartbeat slows and the end feels so fucking close. Every loose end finally being resolved.

“Thanks for doing this,” I tell Mason, ignoring Andrew’s

muted thumps in the trunk as we go over a speed bump and then another.

"No problem," he tells me like I've only asked him to pick up milk on the way home or something.

"I just needed to do something about it all."

"And it's not like he doesn't have it coming to him."

I nod my head and listen to Andrew's muffled screams.

"You sure he's going to be here?" Mason asks me as we pull up to a vacant lot.

Even as we pull up, I can see James inside, moving a curtain in the bedroom.

"Yeah, I'm sure," I tell him.

I know James is here. He's waiting for sentencing and not going anywhere near the city. *He's hiding.*

And I know what that's like.

"You ready?" Mason asks me and I nod my head. "Let's do this."

We'll leave Andrew bound and gagged on James' porch and ring the bell. Or call him or text him. Haven't figured that part out yet. Maybe I'll just knock on the door. It doesn't matter anyway since he already knows someone's here.

A gift from me to him. A truce of sorts.

Sorry I wanted to kill you, here's the fucker who tried first. That sort of thing. I know James knows how to handle a gun and both of us need justice.

Andrew's slamming every which way, but it's 4 a.m. in the suburbs. There isn't another house for nearly half a mile. Even if I took the gag out of his lying mouth, there's no one here but us and James.

I pull out the note as Mason tugs on my shirt and gets my attention.

James is right there in the doorway, rifle ready.

"Just leave him here," I tell Mason and we let Andrew drop to the ground with a muffled scream piercing the air.

I tuck the note in before we drive down the block to make sure James goes and gets him. Which he does. I watch as he reaches down and picks up the scrap of paper and then we drive off.

It's a note that says I'm sorry and that none of this shit should have happened.

They're only words, but they come with revenge wrapped up in a fucking bow.

CHAPTER 32

Kat

It's a truth unyielding,
With death will come life,
Maybe to lessen the sting.

Memories will decay,
But it doesn't stop the sadness,
Nor keep the pain away.

It's not about the ending,
Or the pain from yesterday.
It's always been about the journey,
And the love that's here to stay.

"Do you think he told the cops?" I ask Evan as I pick up the newspaper and read the article.

Samantha got life in prison. Pleaded guilty to multiple murder charges.

James pleaded guilty to his charges as well. But he hasn't been sentenced yet. It's rumored that he gave up information to cut a deal. He'll be out of jail in a year or less according to what the rumor mills are saying. The dealer got off scot-free and now people are saying he skipped town in case more evidence comes in. It pisses me off that he didn't get what he had coming to him, but Evan seems to think the past will catch up to him.

"Told them what exactly?" Evan asks me as he takes a picture frame off the wall of his parents' dining room. He considers it for a moment before grabbing a handful of bubble wrap to package it like he has the others.

The moving company is going to be here tomorrow, but Evan wanted to box up the pictures and a few other things himself.

"That you were there," I say the words quietly, as if it's a dark secret no one can ever know. "With Tony," I add.

Evan shrugs. "He didn't have any proof since we swiped the photos," he says and looks me in the eyes, gauging my reaction as he lowers the wrapped picture into the box.

"And no reason to say anything. He wanted Samantha to go down, and we made that happen." His lips are pressed into a thin line as he makes his way around the table to pull out the chair next to mine.

"You really want to talk about this?" he asks me.

I glance between the article and him, swallowing my words and not knowing how to feel. The entire situation makes me uncomfortable. Worse than that … dreadful.

"I want to know it's going to be okay," I tell him the truth. "I want to make sure *you're* going to be okay."

Evan smirks at me and then leans forward, kissing the tip of my nose, which makes me close my eyes. "You're cute, you know that?" he says.

I reach up quickly to grab his hand and keep him close to me. "I'm serious," I say as I look him in the eyes.

"Baby, I told you there's nothing to worry about," he says as he brushes his hand against my cheek. He pinches my chin between his thumb and forefinger and stares into my eyes. There's a look there that makes me all warm and fuzzy. He's always been able to do that and I love him for it.

"You promise?" I ask him softly and he pecks my lips once then goes in for a deeper one before answering me.

"Well, we do have a baby coming," he says, still staring at my lips. "So I'm sure we've got some things to be worried about, but that mess is over."

The stir of desire drifts away slowly as I peek back down at the article. The picture they chose is one of Samantha giving James a death stare as she was arrested. The papers paint her as a villain and I couldn't be happier.

"And you got that package too," Evan says, bringing my attention back to him. My heart flickers once, then twice as I bite my lip and shrug.

"It was real nice of him," Evan says and I feel the need to smack his arm playfully as he stands up to keep packing.

I place my hand on my belly and tell him, "It was a goodbye and good luck gift from a friend."

"A friend you kissed," Evan reminds me.

"A friend who was there for me when you weren't," I remind him.

His shoulders stiffen a little as he stops midway from taking another photo off the wall. "I know," he says beneath his breath.

"It was a nice gift though, wasn't it?" I ask him.

Evan looks at me with an eyebrow raised and I have to laugh.

"He doesn't have our new address anyway and he didn't put his on the package either."

"Yeah, yeah, yeah," Evan says.

"I really like it." I shrug my shoulders and remember the gift. It's a baby book, called *I'll Love You Forever.* I can't read it without crying.

"It was nice of him, but it better be the last of him," Evan warns me jokingly. I love the trace of a smile on his lips. He knows I'm all his.

I lean back in the chair, and a yawn escapes before I can stop it. I'm halfway to telling him off in some way or another, but the words are stopped.

"You ready to go home?" he asks me and I nod my head but add, "Only if you're all done."

He takes a look around the half-packed house and shakes his head. I have to admit watching him cleaning up his father's place makes my heart hurt.

"You know our baby is going to be tough, right?" he tells me when I start to let the emotions get the best of me.

I rub my swollen bump in smooth circles and pray our baby is okay in there and doesn't know how sad I am in this moment. I just want love for him.

"I hope so," I whisper as Evan comes back over to me. He

wraps his arms around my shoulders and pulls me into his chest. I'm more than grateful as I wrap my arms around him and let my cheek press against his shirt.

"It's true. When a mom goes through hell during pregnancy and handles it as well as you have, the baby can handle anything, you know?"

I let out a sad but genuine laugh into his shirt and try to calm myself down as he rubs my back.

"I hope our baby isn't as emotional as me," I tell him.

"I'm pretty sure you have good reasons, babe," he says and then kisses my hair.

I peek up at him and smile as his lips touch mine.

"And now everything's behind us," he adds.

I feel the need to remind him, "There's good behind us too, isn't there?"

"So much good," he says and then kisses me again before splaying his hand on my belly. "And so much more to come."

EPILOGUE

Kat

Little blips, they come and go,
In rhythm and in time.
Black lines that paint a picture,
And soft lullabies in rhyme.
You're everything, and the reason I need,
To love and to forgive.
My only wish is to keep you safe,
For as long as I shall live.

IT'S REAL. I'm really pregnant. "I can see his heart beat."

"You're so convinced it's a boy?" Evan says although he

doesn't take his eyes off the monitor. A trace of a smile is on his lips and it only grows when the little one moves.

"We'll find out soon," I tell him with a little more glee in my voice.

"Soon as in right now," the doctor says. Dr. Harmony holds the wand right above my belly button. My belly is covered in clear goo and there's more than a little bump now that I'm fifteen weeks along.

I'm quiet as the sound of a steady heartbeat comes through the speaker. Lub-dub, lub-dub, lub-dub. The only thing that distracts me for a moment is Evan taking my hand in his.

"Our little baby," he whispers.

"Your little boy," the doctor corrects him, pointing to the screen. She keeps the wand there for a moment, tapping on the keyboard to take photos and then removes it and the soft, rhythmic heartbeats are gone. But I heard them and that sound will stay with me forever.

"He's healthy?" I ask as my heart swells.

"Perfectly healthy," Dr. Harmony says as she wipes down the equipment and tosses the paper towels into the trash.

"I'll be back in just a bit with some pictures for you two." She has a pretty smile; it's one that reaches her eyes.

"Thank you," Evan and I say in unison.

"A boy," I whisper to him before he cuts me off with a kiss.

"I can't believe we're going to have a son," Evan says, running a hand down his face. "It's real."

"Does it feel real now?" I ask him and he only nods, still looking at the frozen picture on the monitor.

Evan takes my hand again and kisses my knuckles before nodding his head.

My gaze moves from Evan to the screen. The little heart beating in a perfect rhythm.

"I have a feeling it's going to be really, really good," I tell him and get a little choked up.

"It is," Evan says and kisses my hand once more. "I know it is.

Evan

The morning brings a bright light,

Hope and laughter too.

And with time comes a new love,

Faded dreams become anew.

Just remember to hold tight,
And fight for what you love.
For our lost ones will watch over,
And keep us safe from up above.

"WE SHOULD NAME HIM HENRY," Kat says as we walk into the house. Near the Manhattan Bridge is an expensive ass area to live, but the park is so close and this area is where Kat wants to be for our little one, so how could I say no?

She tosses the keys onto the side table, walking past a row of cardboard boxes and a stack of dishes I just brought back from the old place last night. "I've thought a lot about it. And I think we should."

"Henry," I say my father's name and a swell of unexpected emotion catches me off guard. I slip the jacket off my shoulders and move to busy myself, opening the window in the dining room and ignoring the look Kat gives me.

"I know it hasn't been a long time since he passed," Kat says. "It feels like it was yesterday."

She holds her swollen belly and pulls out the head chair in the dining room. At least this room is mostly put together. Kat's nesting has her up all hours and doing shit she shouldn't do. Like carrying heavy boxes and climbing on the furniture to hang curtains.

"I wish he was here," she says and gets teary-eyed. "But we can give him this, you know?"

Her voice is tight with emotion and I nod my head, understanding what she's saying but not liking talking about it.

The wind blows through the house, gently moving the napkins on the table so I'm quick to tuck them into the holder and try to form a response.

"He'd have loved to help us move down here, I think," I tell her.

"At least this time you hired movers," Kat says with a bit of humor, but her voice is solemn.

She winces with pain and grabs a hold of her belly, her eyes closed tight and my heart races.

"Babe?" I ask her and she ignores me. Like she's been doing. For some dumbass reason I keep thinking she'll respond during these Braxton Hicks contractions.

I watch her carefully and walk slowly over to her and wait, afraid to do anything wrong.

I may have fucked up being a good husband, but Pops

showed me how to be a good father and I won't let him down.

"Oh my gosh that was a long one," Kat finally says as her body visibly relaxes.

"Do you want to go in?" I ask her. My nerves are all on edge. I'm fucking terrified, but I won't tell Kat.

She rolls her eyes at me. "For one contraction? I think not."

She reaches into the bag at her feet and pulls out a water bottle. "Besides, I read a baby comes when you're ready and relaxed, and we have four more rooms to set up and get settled in before this little one will be ready. And another two weeks until our due date."

"So what do you think?" she asks me.

"About what?"

"About naming him Henry?" She tilts her head to the side and her long hair falls over her shoulder.

"I think Pops would have loved that," I tell her, taking in a deep breath. "I think he'd be proud."

Lowering myself to the floor in front of her, I let my hands rest on her thighs and bring my forehead down to rest on her belly. "What do you think?" I ask our son and Kat's belly shakes as she laughs.

"You think it's funny, but he's going to know my voice." Kat doesn't hesitate to lean down and kiss me. The first one is a peck, but then she moves her hand to my jaw and keeps me still for a longer one, a deeper one.

It's slow and sensual and makes my blood heat.

"I know he will, and I love you for it."

I take her small hand in mine and look deep into her eyes. She's seen so much of me. All of my bad and the little bit of good I have in me. And she still loves me. There's no way I could doubt that. "I know this year has been rough, but I'm going to do everything I can to make our lives easy for ... forever."

A small smile seems to tickle Kat's lips, still wet from our kiss, and she moves her fingers to them.

"I mean it, Kat. I love you and this baby more than anything." Tears come to my eyes and I only pray she knows that I love her just as much as she loves me.

After a moment, she nods. "I know you do, and I know you will."

I nod my head and move my hand to her belly, feeling our little one kick just beneath the small bit of pressure. It still gets me every time.

"He knows too," Kat says with a smile that lights her eyes.

"So, Henry?" I ask her, feeling a swell of pride in my chest.

She nods her head, her eyes getting glossy as she puts a hand to her belly.

"Henry."

DIARY ENTRY 3

HEY POPS,

I WANTED YOU TO KNOW, every day I think about what I should do to make you proud. Even the days I fuck up. I guess those days especially.

Lately I've been doing good. I think you'd agree. Sometimes I do stupid shit. Like when little Henry peed through his diaper. I changed his diaper but didn't change the onesie. Kat let me have it for that one.

Common sense and all that goes out the window when it comes to him.

He's so small, Pops, I can hold him in one hand. I'm scared I'm gonna break him some days. Kat tells me I'm fine, and that I look good holding him. But I'm so fucking terrified I'm going to mess up.

I guess I'm just nervous to mess up so I keep waiting for her to tell me what to do.

She's taking good care of me. Especially in that department.

She's not going to mess up and that's the only thing that makes me think it's all going to be alright.

Kat's not gonna let me get away with anything anymore.

The best part about that, is that I love it.

I wish I'd listened to you sooner, Pops. I want you to know, I'm trying to make sure my marriage is like yours and Ma's. I know you guys loved each other though and that's what matters.

Thank God for that.

'Cause loving Kat is easy.

I've got to go. I just really wanted to talk to you tonight. Some nights are harder than others and I'm not sure it'll ever get too easy. Even if it does, I'll be thinking of you and wanting your advice.

I LOVE YOU. We all do.

THANK YOU

Thank you for reading Scarred

FOR A LOOK at the rest of the Sins and Secrets Series of Duets and all of my other series and standalone romances, please see my website: www.willowwinter-swrites.com

Printed in the United States
by Baker & Taylor Publisher Services